GAME CHANGE

ALSO BY JOSEPH MONNINGER

Baby

Hippie Chick

Wish

Finding Somewhere

Whippoorwill

GAME CHANGE

Joseph Monninger

HOUGHTON MIFFLIN HARCOURT
BOSTON NEW YORK

FOR SUSAN

hmhbooks.com

Book design by David Futato.
The text was set in Monotype Janson.

The Library of Congress has cataloged the hardcover edition as follows:
Names: Monninger, Joseph, author. Title: Game change / Joseph Monninger.Description: New York, New York : Houghton Mifflin Harcourt, [2019] | Summary: When Zeb Holloway is called to be starting quarterback one week before the state championship game, he realizes he may have a future outside his rural New Hampshire town.
Identifiers: LCCN 2019002041
Subjects: | CYAC: Football—Fiction. | High schools—Fiction. | Schools—Fiction. | Dating (Social customs)—Fiction. | Single-parent families—Fiction. | New Hampshire—Fiction.
Classification: LCC PZ7.M7537 Gam 2019 | DDC [Fic]--dc23 LC record available at https://lccn.loc.gov/2019002041

ISBN: 978-0-544-53122-2 hardcover
ISBN: 978-1-328-59586-7 paperback

Printed in the United States of America
DOC 10 9 8 7 6 5 4 3 2 1
4500764236

Did you think the lion was sleeping because he didn't roar?

—JOHANN CHRISTOPH FRIEDRICH VON SCHILLER

SATURDAY 1

Later, in the week that followed, Zeb Holloway watched the injury form again and again. T. T. Monroe, the finest quarterback ever to play for Rumney High School in Grafton County, New Hampshire, turned the corner on an option play in the last minutes of their win over Hampton, and Zeb knew something had to give.

It was exactly like sensing a wave about to break, and Zeb had turned halfway to check the college scouts in the stands, the men with college baseball hats perched on their heads and slim binocular cords looped around their necks, the ones who came to watch T.T. and time him and smile when they saw him pull off yet another spectacular run or pass—he was a highlight reel, everyone said, and it was true—and by the time Zeb pulled his eyes back, he caught merely the end of T.T.'s leg buckling under him, heard the bone snap, heard T.T. scream like a fox Zeb had once heard scream when his uncle George Pushee had darted an arrow through the animal's cheek.

"No, no, no, no, no," T.T. shouted as soon as the action stopped.

He rolled on the field and grabbed handfuls of grass. Zeb heard the grass rip free of the earth.

"Holloway, warm up!" came the shout.

It was Coach Hoch. Backs coach.

Zeb heard the call far away and did not at first realize it signaled for him to warm up. Then Hawny Spader, his best friend, a third-string defensive back who never played, suddenly appeared with a ball hatched under his arm and his eyes scrambled wide.

"You're going in, man!" Hawny said as if he couldn't believe it even as he gathered the substance of the situation.

Zeb regarded him, trying to pull himself together.

"Holloway! Holloway, get your butt going. Get warmed up!"

Coach Hoch came through the team like a man spreading a shower curtain. Kids jostled away, most of them riveted by the spectacle of T.T. slowly being attended to by the EMTs who now ringed his body. The stadium had gone quiet. Seven thousand people—maybe more, hard to count them, Zeb thought—had turned to stone in an instant. Zeb knew everyone was stunned and he understood the calculation: not only had T.T.'s varsity career suddenly come to a horrible conclusion, but the state championship, the championship that T.T. had promised to bring to the high school on the Saturday after Thanksgiving Day the following week, had now become a long shot. The fans had a difficult time absorbing it all so quickly, Zeb reflected, and the bright flashes of understanding they experienced felt halved and sliced by newer disappointment as the reality of the situation became clearer in each moment that passed.

Before Coach Hoch reached him, Zeb glanced over at the cheerleaders—he looked mostly for Stella, but his eyes couldn't pick her out of the line of pompoms and white sweaters with blue piping that marked the girls' formation. Several of them held their hands to their lips, and then, as if understanding her place in the mourning process was greater than the others', Stella, T.T.'s girlfriend, stepped forward, a bit showy even in this moment of small tragedy, and Zeb saw tears filling her eyes, while two other girls—not ones he knew well—put their arms around her and tried to comfort her. It pained Zeb to admit it, but he could spot the evaluation forming in Stella's movement, her neediness for attention. T.T. was injured, and Stella had become mourner in chief, the girlfriend whose sadness could give her a first starring role. Sad, noble girlfriend. Tragic girlfriend. Zeb knew she would be aware of the new eyes that found her. That was catnip to Stella. She couldn't resist it.

"Forget him now!" Coach Hoch half shouted while he was still yards away. "Forget T.T. We all want him to be okay, that's fine, you can want it to be any which way, but you're the next man up. You hear me? You're the next man up! What do we always say? You're the next man up, that's what we say."

Zeb nodded.

It still hadn't sunk in that he was now to get ready, now to go into the game as T.T.'s replacement.

"I'll warm him up, Coach," Hawny said. "I got him."

"Start throwing," Coach Hoch said. "There you go. Hawny, good man. You get him limbered up, you hear? Now quit looking at T.T. There's not a thing in the world you can do for him. No,

I take that back. What you can do for him, Zeb, what you can do is step in and finish the game the way it's supposed to be finished. You hear? Zeb, you tracking with me?"

Zeb nodded, his stomach buzzing with butterflies. He had been in a game only once the entire season, in a mop-up victory over Campton when the score had been so lopsided the game had taken on a festive air for the Rumney team. His role had been meaningless, a mere comic piece of punctuation because the game had been so securely put on ice by T.T. Even this game against Hampton, halfway through the fourth quarter, was iced. By rights, T.T. should have come out before, and he probably would have after the final series, but Zeb knew some of it had been to parade for the college scouts what T.T. could do. It had been showing off, honestly, and Zeb didn't like thinking it, but he knew his grandmother in Maine would say something about the Lord and pride going before a fall.

Still dazed, he stepped back and grabbed the ball when Hawny underhanded it to him. He tossed it to Hawny, putting some air underneath it. Hawny caught it, tucked it close to his body as receivers were trained to do, and lofted it back.

"Okay, now, nothing fancy," Coach Hoch said, finding his calmer voice, his sincere voice. Coach Hoch stood next to Zeb, sideways. He was a solid, thick man, with lips turned too wide up and down, a fish with its lips pressed against the side of an aquarium. "We're golden in this game. We'll be running the ball and taking it slow. Grind out the clock, that's all we have to do. We'll hand the game to our defense . . . that's it. Not a thing to worry about. What does Coach K say? It's a game and it's supposed to be fun. Isn't that what he says?"

Zed nodded. That was, indeed, what Coach K said.

For a moment, Zeb concentrated on throwing. He could always throw. In fact, although he was not as explosive as T.T., not nearly as fast or elusive, he sometimes felt that as a thrower, a pure passer measured by that standard alone, he could hold his own with T.T. Zeb lived to throw, whereas T.T. passed merely as a part of his arsenal. For Zeb, passing constituted his only football gift. Even now, lobbing the ball to Hawny and catching it when it came back, Zeb took satisfaction in the motion, in the quiet tick of the laces as they left his right hand. He threw a good, tight spiral. Hawny, on receiving the ball, nodded and tossed the ball back. They had played catch a thousand times, but never quite like this, never with the game open and waiting.

"Throw a couple hard . . . that's it . . . don't wait for the game to come to you. You look good. You've got this. Keep your head about you. You got to meet the game, right? Isn't that right?"

"That's right, Coach," Zeb answered.

"Okay, they got him up. Okay. Here we go. Nice and easy does it. Here we go. You're in good hands, Zeb. You don't have to win the thing all by yourself. Just nice and level. That's the boy."

The EMTs had secured an inflatable cast around T.T.'s leg. The cast looked out of place, a pool toy in an otherwise serious world. The crowd clapped, but it wasn't the usual roar T.T. received, not half of it. T.T waved from the flat bed of a golf cart as it puttered toward the locker room.

Coach K's long left arm slowly settled around Zeb's shoulders. It felt awkward being so close to the man, to the legendary coach with four state championships and the grim, serious demeanor of a person who did not for an instant question his own authority. Zeb fought the impulse to shake the man's arm off his shoulders. Coach K had never shared such intimacy with him before; there were times, in fact, when Zeb wondered if Coach K knew who he was.

"Now just settle down. These are your glory days, just like the song says. Believe on that. I know your heart's beating fast, but there's no reason to give into it, you hear me? Lean into your practice and your fundamentals. Stick to your fundamentals."

Zeb heard him but was more astonished by the powerful bad breath coming from Coach K. Zeb nodded. Nodding almost always provided whatever it was adults seemed to need from him. He nodded again. This time he knew it had been too much, too transparent, because Coach K pushed him a little away and regarded him carefully with his pale blue eyes.

"You'll be okay, Zeb," Coach K said. "This is a moment. This is what we practice for, you understand? This is why we drill and why we do two-a-days in August. You reading me, son? When the time to perform has arrived, the time to prepare has passed."

Zeb nodded, recognizing one of the thousand quotes the coach liked to throw into his conversations. He slowly comprehended that Coach K required more of a reply, a spoken acknowledgment.

"Yes, sir."

"You look around, now. You see this stadium? They're all pulling for you. Every last one . . . at least on our side. They're sending you good thoughts, you hear?"

"Yes, sir."

"Now, what we want to do is simply possess the ball and eat time. Tell the backs to stay inbounds. Tell the line we need crisp blocking in this series. You got it?"

"Yes, sir."

"Zeb, you remember when you were a little boy and just went into the backyard or wherever it was you played? Well, it's the same game. Have fun with it. Enjoy it and let it shine through you, okay?"

Zeb nodded hard and started onto the field, but Coach K grabbed his arm and nearly jerked him off his feet.

"You need a play, right?" Coach K said.

Zeb nodded. His mouth felt white inside and dry.

"You go twins right, Twenty-Seven Boom. You run it that way, then run it back the other way. Bread and butter. Make them stop us. Nothing fancy, no complicated formations. Twenty-Seven Boom. Now go ahead. Tell the backs to keep both hands on the ball."

Running onto the field, Zeb had to keep himself from turning to look for the source of the crowd's applause. They applauded for him, he realized an instant later, just in time to save himself from the embarrassment of looking. They applauded not for anything he had done, of course, but for a general sense of relief that T.T.'s slot had been filled by a willing, if lesser, backup. Mixed in with it, he guessed, was a measure of speculation about what this kid could do, what he might bring to the game that T.T. had not. That was absurd, naturally. He could bring to the game nothing that T.T. could not bring, and in confirmation of this thought, he saw two of the college scouts rise from their seats and snatch their butt pillows off the aluminum bleachers. They were not here to see him, obviously, and although that should have made Zeb feel slightly better—after all, it was less pressure to perform—it only made him feel more of an impostor.

"Here he comes, here comes the man," someone from the offensive circle said. Zeb could not identify the voice, but he was grateful for it.

"Next man up," someone else shouted. "Pick 'em up, pick 'em up. Next man."

Zeb looked at the huddle as he approached, his wind knocking hard in his chest. He needed to calm down. He needed to get perspective. He pictured himself in a deer stand sometime in early December, say, up near the Dummer Camp with his uncle Pushee and his uncle's buddy Whoopie. He pictured his breath coming out slow and steady, like a train—Uncle Pushee always said, *Like a train sitting in the station and waiting to go*—until the cold and the sight of a deer stepping softly, softly through the forest brought him slightly forward, hawk-necked and keen, with the slide of the arrow nocking back against the compound bow creating a sound like foil being pulled off its roll just before it's ripped on the ragged teeth.

"Call a play, man, call a play," Dunham said.

Dunham the fullback.

Then Zeb flexed to one knee and looked up at the faces bent over to watch him.

"Twenty-Seven Boom," he said, "break."

The team broke, but then Jiler, the center, asked loud enough for everyone to hear: "What's it on?"

Meaning "When do you hike the ball?" Meaning not even one play in and Zeb already felt like a dumb ass.

"On two," Zeb yelled. "On two."

Jiler nodded, the red dot of blood on the bridge of his nose

—which was permanently raw throughout the season—shaking a single drop of the red clotted fluid to the bulge of his right nostril. He nodded and hustled away, then stuck his butt in the air and waited. They should have practiced a few snaps, Zeb realized, but it was too late for that. He tried to appear calm as he followed the offensive line to the scrimmage. He had seldom run plays with the starting team, certainly never in real conditions, and it felt as if he had been given the controls of a first-class machine the working of which he did not quite understand.

The Hampton linebacker Tiny Crawford—Zeb knew about him from the pregame talks with Coach Hoch and T.T.—slobbered a few commands to his defense, then danced forward as if he wanted to jump over the line and jerk Zeb's head from his shoulders.

"Coming after you, sub. You hear me? I'll get you, my pretty."

Zeb saw the linebacker smile.

Then, as if the words came from a second mouth inside him, Zeb said, "Set, ready, hut, hut . . ."

The ball came into his hands.

It came smoothly and he took it and spun and stuck his arm out to Otzman, the team's best running back—besides T.T.—and Otzman snapped it away with a huff and folded it into his gut. Zeb continued the fake, that was his job, and pretended to bootleg around the left end. No one believed he had the ball, but that was okay, it was protocol, and he hardly saw Otzman run into a mass of bodies at the line of scrimmage, going nowhere, and a ref blew a whistle to signal the end of the play.

Zeb trotted back to the forming huddle.

"Okay, listen," he said, trying to take command as he knew a quarterback should, "we don't want to go out of bounds. Backs, two hands on the ball. We want to keep the clock going. Line, you got to be crisp . . ."

"Just call the freaking play," McCay said.

He was the right guard, a smallish, stumpy kid with a neck like a donkey's.

Zeb called the Boom play to the other side.

"On one," he remembered to say.

The team clapped in unison. They broke from the huddle as they had been trained to break since September 1.

"Coach K wants to see you upstairs," Coach Hoch said. "Hop along, now. Don't keep the man waiting."

Zeb nodded.

He wore his game pants and a Rumney T-shirt, and he still had his shoulder pads crouched on his shoulders. He stripped off the shoulder pads and tossed them in his locker. The floor, when he walked across it barefoot, felt sticky and slick at the same time. Sticky, he knew, from the balls of ankle tape that clotted the areas around the benches; slick, doubtless, from the streams of water that trailed the players as they came out of the showers in white towels, their bodies pink from the cold air outside and the blood the steamy water brought out.

Zeb climbed the stairs, trying his best to stay calm. He did not like going upstairs. The upstairs belonged to the coaches and training staff; as a rule, going upstairs meant you were hurt or in trouble. He didn't fit either category, so he felt a bit at sea. As he reached the top step, he smelled onions. Someone had set out a pile of hoagies, and three boosters—local men with business connections—held plates in front of them. It felt hot and Zeb halted, orienting himself, then finally spotted Coach K. Dino Puglasi, the chubby manager with a round, full moon face, kneeling at the coach's feet, unlacing the man's cleats. Coach K had a bad back and it wasn't uncommon to see Dino helping him.

"Are you hungry, son?" one of the boosters asked before Zeb could think or move.

"No, sir, thank you."

"You sure? They're from Ginger's . . . best subs in town."

"No, thank you, sir."

The man nodded and made a tiny toast with his corner of sandwich. Zeb saw Coach K wiggle his finger to call him over.

"Have a seat," Coach K said, sliding a straight-backed chair over. "You did a nice job today."

"Thank you, Coach," Zeb said, sitting down carefully.

Dino finished with the shoes and carried them off. Coach K lifted each foot slowly and massaged his toes for a minute.

"You did what we asked," Coach K said, then called to Dino for a sub.

"Ham?" Dino asked.

Coach K nodded. "You sure you don't want a sandwich, Zeb?" Coach K asked.

"I'm positive, sir."

"You're a polite kid. I like that. It's a compliment to your upbringing."

Zeb didn't say anything. He had to concentrate on staying level. Coach K looked tired. He looked older, too, as if the season had drained something from him. Pictures of him in the paper always made him appear bigger, Zeb decided. In person, Coach K looked smaller, a halfback, maybe, or a defensive safety. His eyes, Zeb knew, set Coach K apart. They were pale blue, dull, but somehow more penetrating than the eyes of any other human Zeb had met. The kids on the team called it his "tractor beam" and Zeb agreed with the assessment. You could not get free of the eyes once they grabbed onto you. Coach K read books on warfare and tactical arrangement, and more than once he'd quoted generals or Chinese priests in his pregame pep talk. He believed especially in eye contact and directness.

"Anyway," Coach K said, accepting the sandwich Dino held out, "T.T.'s at the hospital now, so we don't know the final verdict, but I think it's safe to say he won't be back. Darn shame, that's a given. He's had a heck of a year, as you know."

"Yes, sir, he has. Sorry to hear that."

"Right now you're the second man on the depth chart. That means you're the starting quarterback for the time being. Do you have any problem with that?"

Coach K looked directly at him. Zeb forced himself to meet the man's eyes, although he wondered what Coach meant by *the time being.*

"I have no problem with that, Coach."

"We'll be looking at our options very carefully," Coach K said after a moment. He bit into his sandwich and chawed it in his right cheek. "We have a week to prepare. That's not much time. You need to be honest with me, now. Are you as up on the playbook as you should be?"

"I think so, sir."

"Think so or know so?"

"I know so."

"Good. That's a good attitude. That's the right attitude. What I need you to do is take another look at the playbook and see if there's anything you don't get. Now's not the time to fake anything. We're playing for the state championship next Saturday. We understanding each other on that?"

"Yes, sir."

"You throw well, but you need to be in charge out there. We'll work on that next week. You need to work on your ball handling too. Your teammates need to see you as a leader. Is that clear?"

Zeb nodded.

"This is something you'll remember all your life, son. State championship game. Guys," Coach K said, raising his voice and preparing to take another bite of his sandwich, "will Zeb here remember the game next Saturday all his life or what?"

The man who had offered Zeb a sandwich said in a loud voice, "You better freaking believe it. All your life."

"Good or bad, you're going to remember it, Zeb. Now go home and get some rest. Take it easy this weekend."

"Yes, sir."

"Rest and catch up on your sleep. Take care of yourself. You just became extremely important to a whole lot of people. I hope you know that. You're not in this alone. The whole town is counting on you. Remember, victory begins in the heart."

Zeb stood. Coach K bit into his sandwich and began chewing, a single wayward onion dropping onto his chest. Dino swung by with a steaming cup of black coffee. Zeb nodded to him. Dino nodded back.

"It's a complete pisser," Hawny Spader said from behind the wheel of his lifted F-150. "You, the starting QB? Insane. I love it. Playing for the state championship, and who's the starting QB? You got it. One Zebulon Holloway!"

Hawny sat forward on the bench seat of the Ford F-150. He was a short, compact kid, with a blond buzzcut and the kind of skin that let you see the veins beneath it. He loved his F-150, and he had outfitted it with risers as soon as he got it so he could look down on cars and people around him. *A short man's truck,* Zeb's uncle Pushee always said. Hawny didn't care what people said about his truck, Zeb knew, because Hawny loved it like a person might love a horse or a dog. He had tricked it out so that it ran a big spoiler in front; it had mud flaps with Yosemite Sam shooting at whoever followed behind and a claxon horn that played "La Cucaracha" whenever Hawny felt the need to hear it. The only thing it lacked, in fact, was a radio or sound system, because Hawny's dad said a bunch of music blaring would only distract Hawny and cause his death. Zeb wasn't sure Hawny's dad wasn't right about that.

Hawny drove down Woodland, then crossed over to Holton Street.

"I still can't believe you played," Hawny said. "You *played,* man! You looked good, you know? I mean, you looked like you were a player and you were playing . . ."

"I forgot to call the snap count on the very first play."

"So?" Hawny asked, turning. "So what? So you made a mistake.

So what? People make mistakes, but you came in and did what you needed to do. We won, right? Next week is your week, kiddo."

"I'm a backup, Hawny. Let's not get crazy."

"You're a backup who's playing in a state championship game. Get that into your head. And the whole damn town is going to be bowing to you. You know how crazy this gets. They already have signs up all over! Are you nuts? You just hit the lottery, man!"

Zeb shook his head, trying to get his mind around it. Hawny had a point and the whole thing seemed dreamlike. Zeb felt an inner pleasure that he didn't quite recognize. Things seldom went his way. It almost brought a smile to his lips, almost, and to obscure it he punched Hawny softly on the arm.

"What if you got in too?" he asked Hawny, taking cover in a question as he sometimes did. "What if you got in, and we lit it up? I'd throw it to you no matter what. You could have ten guys on you and I would just bomb it out there and see what happens."

"No way I'm getting in," Hawny said. "I'm going to finish my career at good old Rumney High without playing a single down."

"They should put you in for a kickoff or something. It sucks that they don't."

"Maybe they would, but not for the state championship. Don't go dreaming on me. I kind of don't even want to go in anymore. It's like a point of pride with me now."

"It's not right they don't put you in sometime. I mean, you practice as much as anyone. You're like the king of the nut squad."

Hawny shrugged. Zeb couldn't help feeling he should share some of what he had just won with Hawny, though he didn't know how that was possible.

"How about T.T.? That leg is wankered," Hawny said, drawing

up behind a car near the light on Ellwood Ave. "I couldn't even look at it. It's bent all to hell. Got to put him out on the icebergs for the polar bears, man. He's done for."

"I should go over and see him in the hospital."

"Good luck with that. What are you doing tomorrow?"

"I've got to work in the morning. Then Uncle Pushee talked about going out for deer."

"Up to Dummer?"

"I think so."

"He already got one, right?"

"Muzzleloader. He works it so he can get three. He wants to make sure I use my tag, otherwise he'll jack one."

"Uncle Pushee is hard core, man."

Uncle Pushee *was* hard core, Zeb agreed. But his mind didn't want to focus on deer or Uncle Pushee.

"I keep thinking of T.T.," he said. "I mean, he's got everything going for him. Great athlete, college scouts, you name it. He dates one of the prettiest girl in school—"

"You think Stella is hot? I mean, really hot? I never thought she was all that," Hawny said, moving when the light turned and swinging onto Cowherd Lane. "She knows that she's good-looking and acts stuck up."

Hawny was right about Stella. She was aware of her looks. Whenever Zeb hung around her, he noticed she always found a way to see herself in the mirror or any reflecting surface at all. Sometimes being near her felt like sharing a scene in a movie she starred in and directed herself. Zeb could never tell if he felt attracted to her or sorry for her. He imagined it was something in between.

"She's a little needy," Zeb said, defending her. "She just wants attention."

"Listen to you!" Hawny said. "You going all psychobabble on me. You got a thing for Stella? You going to take T.T.'s position and his girlfriend in the same week? That's just not right!"

"No, I just mean, Stella is okay. Sometimes we talk. Don't get all weird on me. Don't make it into something it's not."

"Oh, she has depth, eh? Is that what you're saying? She's a star-fucker, Zeb. She's with T.T. only because he's the big dog on campus. But you got all kinds of surprises lined up, don't you? T.T. would kick your ass, you know, if you mess with Stella? He'd take his cast off or whatever he has on his leg and beat you silly. Those two are like male and female versions of the same person."

Hawny was right about that too. T.T. had already asked a time or two about the conversations Zeb had occasionally with Stella. Zeb couldn't tell if T.T. was jealous or merely annoyed with Stella for needing so much attention. Either way, it wasn't a line Zeb had any interest in crossing.

"Coach K has some serious bad breath," Zeb said to change the subject.

"Does he? I never got close enough to know."

"It's epically bad."

"Gross. You working tonight?" Hawny asked, banking a turn onto Brick Street.

"Nope. Not tonight."

"That's good. The star quarterback ought to be kicking back!"

"I'm hardly a star quarterback."

"You never know. You might make it rain out there. You got to get into this thing, Zeb. Great opportunities come to those who make the most of small ones. Isn't that what Coach K always says? You're like Tommy Brady! Drew Bledsoe just got hurt and you're coming into the game!"

"Maybe. Or maybe I'm about to make a fool of myself."

"Nah. You're solid, man. You suddenly became the most famous guy in Rumney Township. You got to get your head around this. This is freaking enormous, dude."

Zeb smiled. Hawny always had a different take on things. That was one of the features of Hawny's personality that Zeb admired. He was goofy, but good goofy. And in some part of himself, Zeb understood this opportunity was big. A lot of people would be watching, for better or worse.

"Stella, eh?" Hawny said when he finally pulled into Zeb's driveway. "She *is* bait. And she is wicked tight."

"And she's T.T.'s girlfriend."

"Dangerous territory, man. You better be careful."

Zeb climbed out. Cold air moved over him and he felt it suck down into his body. He kept the door open while he reached in the back of Hawny's pickup for his bag of clothes. It felt good and warm in Hawny's truck and he almost hated to leave it. Behind him, Uncle Pushee's house was dark.

"Thanks, man," Zeb said to Hawny.

"I'm hanging with the starting quarterback of the Rumney Raiders. I'll drive you anywhere you want this week. The week after that, you're back to being old Zebulon Holloway, half-ass grease monkey. You'll be yesterday's news."

"You want to go over with me to see T.T.?"

"Would he come to see me if I were hurt? Not thinking so. He doesn't know who I am. I'm just a nut-squadder to him. No, thanks. I'm not going to pretend we're buddies now just because he's hurt."

"He's your teammate. That should count for something."

"He doesn't give a flying deuce about me and you know it."

Zeb shrugged. He couldn't disagree. He nodded his chin at Hawny and closed the door. He smelled truck exhaust as Hawny backed out. Hawny hit "La Cucaracha" as he pulled away. He always did.

It was cold in the old Sunline camper that Zeb lived in with his mother. His mother, Janey, hadn't been home all day. She hadn't been back last night either, so the fire had gone out in the Jøtul and the camper felt cold as well water.

Zeb swung his backpack down on the couch and turned on the center overhead light. He stood for a second glancing around. It didn't look great in the camper. He saw that. He understood he was partially to blame for the mess, but some of it, a lot of it, came from his mom. She collected things, mostly ridiculous things, whacky little knickknacks she hauled back from thrift shops and yard sales. She had just found a new store over by the Rumney diner, and for the past week or so she had been splurging her tip money on porcelain dolls and puppy-dog figurines. She loved them. It boxed him up to think about it.

He grabbed a copy of the *PennySaver* from the stack on the counter and broke a couple pine twigs across his knee. Then he opened the Jøtul and laid up the fire, crumpling paper and twigs together in a hash, fitting in a hunk of birch as a firedog. He had to get up and look around for matches. It occurred to him as he lifted from his knee—probably because it was the same motion he used after calling a play and breaking the huddle—that he was the starting quarterback of the Rumney Raiders. For the briefest moment he felt something warm and proud build inside of him. He wasn't T.T., didn't possess even half of T.T.'s stunning ability, but he stood for a second and looked out the window and caught his reflection staring back at him. He couldn't bring himself to smile, exactly, but he felt a deep, heavy satisfaction continue to fill him, and to his surprise his eyes filled with tears. He wished, somehow, that he had someone to tell. He thought of his mother and thought of Uncle Pushee, but they wouldn't understand the news in the way he needed someone to understand. They would say it was great, good, way to go, but they considered playing sports a waste of time mostly. Uncle Pushee was fond of saying that the Saturday he spent watching a bunch of boys playing a game and taking it for entertainment was the day he was ready to be carried to heaven. Uncle Pushee wasn't the one to tell about being the quarterback in a state championship game, that was certain. It was a taste Zeb had to have just to himself.

As Zeb knelt before the stove again, he realized who he did want to tell: *Stella.* She would understand. She loved TV shows that let common people show off their talents. It didn't matter if the people did better or worse than the audience anticipated; she simply liked that they had a chance. She watched all of those shows. Underneath it, Zeb understood Stella waited for her chance somehow. She wanted to get out and get going with her life. She thought her prettiness would carry her someplace, but Zeb wasn't sure she could depend on it as a ticket.

Anyway, that's who he wanted to tell. He wanted to tell Stella.

He struck the match and held the flame to the crumpled paper.

He shook his head a little to clear it. Life had some wicked-fast turns, he thought as he touched the match to the paper in three different spots. He tossed the match onto the paper and leaned back to watch the flame climb. It would be an hour, he knew, before the stove chased the cold out of the camper.

With one eye on the stove, he fixed himself a bowl of tomato soup, crushed a half dozen saltines on top, and carried it to the rocking chair that his mother kept close to the stove. He sat down and felt a loop of weariness circle him. If he put his head back, and if the stove continued to throw heat, he would be asleep before he finished his supper. He forced himself to sit forward and ate the soup. After a while he dug into his pocket and pulled out his phone. He checked his messages, then went to the Rumney Raiders Facebook page. The page had more than seventeen thousand followers, and the buzz had already begun about T.T.'s injury. A few people asked how serious it was, and others—some names he recognized—came right back and said T.T. was done for the season. He read through maybe thirty threads before he saw a mention of his own name. In answer to *Who was the backup,* someone had typed, *Zeb Holloway, three-year bench rider.*

He's no T.T., someone else wrote.

No one is T.T. Not in the entire country.

Coach K will get Holloway ready.

Coach K can stand on his head, Holloway ain't no T.T.

Then someone asked about Merrymeeting, their opponent in the state championship game, and the thread went down that rabbit hole for more responses than Zeb could count. He clicked his phone off when he heard his mother open the door.

"Heyyyyy," she called.

That's how she always called. Her voice sounded like it wasn't sure if it wanted to say hello or goodbye. He listened to her drop her things. Her keys went first, then her coat. She kicked off her shoes last. They hit against the walls and he heard her slide her feet into her slippers.

"How was it?" she asked, simultaneously holding up a pair of porcelain Franciscan monks for him to examine. She wiggled them to make them dance. Then she put them on the window ledge beside a black sheep and a tawny river otter. She still wore her brown waitress uniform. Her restaurant was called the Captain's Table.

"Okay," he said. "It went okay."

"Did you win?" she asked, pulling back from the window ledge. "I tried to find the score on the radio, but I couldn't get it to come in. I wish they would get a decent radio station for the games. These mountains cut off every station around here."

"We won."

She stepped back and examined the row of porcelain figures.

"Salt- and peppershakers," she said. "The monks, I mean. They can be valuable. I got them for a steal."

He nodded. He understood she needed to feel she'd won sometimes, that she'd tricked someone, gotten a deal to answer all the beat-downs she took in her life, but it was the wrong game and the wrong thing to match herself against. Still, it wasn't anything you could say to her. He watched as she reached forward and arranged the spacing between the two monks to match the spacing around the other figurines. When she was satisfied, she stepped away and moved in front of the stove.

"God, it's cold in here," she said. "Did you just get back?"

He nodded. She pointed her chin at his bowl.

"Good, I'm glad you're having soup. It's a soup kind of day, isn't it? I may have a bowl myself."

"How did you do?"

"A hundred seventeen."

"Not bad."

"They don't tip in that restaurant. They just don't. I talked to Kelly the other day about her restaurant . . . the Greenhouse? She makes a hundred bucks at brunch on Sunday! She makes twice that in, like, two hours during dinner."

"Hey, could I borrow the car tonight?" he asked, knowing a quick change of topic often worked on her. Given too much time, she found a world of objections to almost anything he proposed.

"For how long?"

"Just an hour or so."

"Well, I guess. I might have an invitation to go out tonight."

"Wouldn't whoever it is drive you, then?"

"You know who it is, Zeb. It's Arthur."

"Can't Arthur give you a ride?"

She shrugged. Her social life always had complications, he knew. Crackups and make-backs and who knew what all. Mostly it revolved around going to the Fish Bowl for margaritas, but how she got there, and where she went afterward, he didn't usually let himself consider. Arthur was fairly steady except when he wasn't. He had thin hair and a muscled build that had gone a little to fat. He resembled a cake that someone had overfrosted, but he was usually pretty okay about his mother. Zeb got along with Arthur all right.

A spark from the stove snapped and shot up. It made a pretty little arc before it landed in front of his mom. She stepped on it and put it out. The cinder created a black smudge on the floor. When she was sure she had extinguished the spark, she turned around and shut the stove door.

"Warmer now," she said.

"Is Uncle Pushee home? Is his truck over there?"

"I don't think so. What do you need him for?"

"I'm supposed to work for him tomorrow."

"Thought you were going deer hunting."

"Work first, I think."

"Well, if you're working tomorrow, make sure you put some gas in the car, you hear? You don't get to keep all your money while I spend mine on groceries."

"I will."

He thought then about telling her his news. He thought about explaining that something big had happened, but he couldn't get his tongue to carve out the sort of air he needed to carry it to her ears. She would try to be enthusiastic, he knew, and that would only make it worse. The rest of the week he would be forced to endure a bunch of questions and comments, little mom-interrogations, and he didn't think he could stand that. In his experience, it seldom paid to volunteer information. It was better to let the world drift to you.

"I'm going to fix a drink," she said, moving away from the stove toward the kitchen counter. "You go ahead if you want, take the car, but not far, right? We depend on that car, Zeb."

"I know, Mom."

"Please be careful. There's no fat on the bone, Zeb."

She combed his hair back with her hand. She tapped her finger lightly on the center of his forehead for emphasis. *No fat on the bone;* he got it. They never had fat on the bone, so he wasn't certain why she needed to point it out. She squatted and kissed his hairline quickly, and pretty soon afterward the ice trays cracked.

Holloway has a decent arm.
He's a second-string QB. You be dreaming, dude.
What time does the game start?
They haven't posted it. Probably a.m.
T.T. is better on one leg than Holloway on two.
Maybe T.T. can play on crutches.

Plymouth Regional Hospital was a beige, unassuming building. When Zeb parked his mom's Honda Civic at the back edge of the lot, he shook his head, thinking of T.T. being here in a drab little hospital room. T.T. hated smalltime, hated New Hampshire for its ruralness, and it was a cruel irony that he ended up here tonight instead of being out enjoying a fancy dinner somewhere courtesy of one of the visiting college recruiters. T.T. would not be happy.

Zeb cupped his hand over his mouth and blew into it, checking his breath. He pulled the collar of his flannel shirt tighter against his neck, then tucked his hands into the front pouch of his Raiders sweatshirt. He wondered as he pushed through the visitors' door if he was overstepping by visiting T.T. They weren't great friends, but they had been fellow quarterbacks for three years. They had performed all their drills together, studied film side by side, checked each other's arms out at the end of each summer to see what the other had become. Zeb felt fairly solid that his motive for visiting centered somewhere on those considerations; they were friends, and he hoped T.T. would see it that way. Zeb would not allow his mind to go to Stella. That wasn't why he wanted to pay a visit. He could say that honestly.

"Hey, 's'up?" T.T. said when Zeb finally found the right room after wandering the hallways for a couple minutes. Half a dozen people crowded around the bed. T.T. sat against a pillow, his leg hoisted up as if he needed to follow through from kicking a field goal. The cast, Zeb observed, looked enormous. It was not a minor-injury cast, he didn't think. No question about that. Zeb stood for a moment, unsure of what to do. The people around T.T.'s bed fanned out a little, as if T.T. rested in the dead center of the flaring neck of a cobra. Zeb smiled and tried to shrink back, but he was committed. He didn't see any of their teammates.

"How are you feeling?" Zeb asked, standing awkwardly at the foot of T.T.'s bed. "You in much pain?"

"He's all right, everything considered," a large woman said. "We pray to the Lord to restore His gifts to T.T."

It was T.T.'s mom. She was a keg-ish, thick woman, wearing a blue dress that had a shimmer under the hospital lighting. Something about the way people had gathered around T.T. made Zeb wonder if he had interrupted a prayer. A Bible rested on the bed next to T.T.'s injured leg. The Bible looked like a tiny trapdoor leading down into the covers.

"Yes, ma'am," Zeb said, collecting himself. "We all hope that."

"It's hard, man," T.T. said. "My leg is shot. I still can't believe it. I wasn't even hit."

"Sorry, T.T. It's a lousy break."

"Put your faith in the Lord, T.T.," his mom said. "All things are the property of the Lord. The Lord gives and the Lord takes. It's not our right to ask why. We rest our lives in His palm, in health and in sickness."

T.T. nodded. Zeb met T.T.'s eyes. T.T. didn't seem confident that all things flowed from the Lord or whatever his mother had just said. Zeb saw that much.

"So this is your backup," T.T.'s dad said from the other side of the bed. "I just put it together. I had trouble placing this boy . . . Zeb, right? You're a Holloway, aren't you?"

"Yes, sir."

"Well, good on you for stopping in to see your friend. You're the first teammate that's come by. The coaches came right after the game. Coach K and everyone. The whole crew."

"I only wish he could play on Saturday," Zeb said, because something like that—some sort of phrase of consolation—was expected of him. "For states, I mean."

"His season's over, that's for sure," the man said. "But there will be other seasons, won't there, T.T.?"

"Yes, sir."

Zeb felt the neck of the cobra begin to constrict. The people on either side of the bed began shutting the circle. T.T. started to fade. His eyes closed and he looked, suddenly, more like a child than a young man. T.T.'s mom put her fingers to her lips and came and took Zeb's arm. She walked him out.

"Bless you for stopping in," she said. "He's tired. He's a tired, tired boy right now. It's been an emotional day for him. And the pain."

Zeb nodded.

"Have you been saved, young man?"

"Not so you would know it."

The woman surprised him by laughing. It wasn't a phony, polite laugh. It came from deep down.

"You're an honest boy. I asked because we can use your prayers. We had so much hope for T.T. and now this . . ."

Zeb nodded. He didn't know if he could pray for T.T., or for anyone, really, but he understood the desire to pray.

"I'll try," Zeb said, starting down the hallway. "Nice meeting you."

"Nice of you to stop in. Not everyone did."

"I think it's early. They'll come by, I'm pretty sure."

The woman nodded and turned and went back inside. Zeb walked down a wide set of stairs, not sure if he had told the woman the truth. People had mixed feelings about T.T. The fact was, T.T. was a black kid in a nearly all-white school—in a nearly all-white state—and he couldn't help being the center of attention. *People watched him.* Anytime the question of race came up in a class—reading *Huckleberry Finn,* for instance, or discussing Black Lives Matter in social studies—everyone turned to T.T. Even the teachers. By being black, T.T. had to be the spokesman for anything race-related, which was nutty and unfair, Zeb knew, but there it was. Added to that was T.T.'s talent. He was a genuinely superb athlete, a QB listed in *Scholastic News* as one of the top five recruits for colleges in America. The rumor was he had already committed to USC on a full ride. Sometimes he could come across as arrogant or conceited, but Zeb could hardly blame him. He really was that good, but some guys on the team found him too cocky for their liking. They had to respect him, for sure, but plenty of guys wouldn't be entirely disappointed to see T.T. get taken down a peg or two.

Zeb was glad to step outside and breathe fresh air. He stood for a moment in the bright light of the visitors' entrance and felt again the pleasure of being the quarterback for the New Hampshire state championship game. But the pleasure came on a wash of guilt, because here he was, not a hundred yards away from T.T.'s hospital bed, smiling over being a starting quarterback at last.

He still stood under the visitors' entrance when Stella's car drove past.

He thought maybe he should leave, but he couldn't make himself go. It took her a while to climb out of the car. When she did, she had a Dunkin' Donuts iced coffee in her hand.

"Hi, Zeb," Stella said. "Have you been up already?"

"I just came down."

"How's he doing?"

"He's sleepy. I guess they have him pretty sedated."

"I can't believe this is happening. Right before his last game."

"I know. It's a shame."

Stella took a sip of her iced coffee. Zeb noticed the straw's top was red from her lipstick.

"How are you feeling about it all? You're suddenly the quarterback for the state championship game. That's got to get your butterflies going."

"I don't think I've quite got my head around it yet."

"All those people counting on you? It would make me jumpy, I can tell you that. Some of the cheerleaders asked me about you. You're suddenly on their radar. Bethy and Maddie think you're cute."

"It's just a game. And nobody thinks I'm cute, Stella. That's just you pretending."

"You think so? You'll see," she said, taking the straw again. The ice cubes in the coffee swirled like ghosts. "You're the quarterback for a state championship game. Do you even get how big that is?"

"I guess. I don't know. It's hard to take in."

Stella smiled. He realized, maybe for the first time, how sharply people would watch him this next week. Truly watch him. It didn't make him nervous, exactly, just on edge and ready. He couldn't let himself think about it too much. He knew Coach K would keep the game plan simple. That's what the fans wouldn't know. The Raiders wouldn't be pulling anything fancy. Mostly Zeb had to game-manage and try to sneak the Raiders ahead for a touchdown and then let the defense hold them. If the game had been on his shoulders, *really* on his shoulders, he would have felt much more concerned. He had to keep himself steady inside his excitement.

"Well, I should get up there," Stella said. "If it gets too crazy this week, let me know. We can talk or whatever."

"Thanks. I appreciate that."

"You'll do great. T.T. always said you could throw better than he did, and coming from T.T., that's saying a lot. He would never admit something like that if it weren't true. He hates to admit anyone is better at anything than he is."

"Well, I don't know about that."

"You think he's lying? Or that I'm lying?" Stella asked with a twinkle.

"I meant about me being a better thrower," Zeb said.

"You're too humble, Zeb. This isn't your week to be humble."

Then Stella put her hand on his forearm. She meant it, he imagined, to encourage him, to say that this was his week, except it sent such a tingle through him that he almost couldn't stand it. He curled his arm quickly and touched her sleeve and she turned away and then turned back and looked at him.

After the hospital, he drove to Meater Lake. It was a place to go, nothing special, but he parked and climbed out of the car. He checked his phone, but the reception wasn't good. The cold air pushed at him. He sat on the front fender of the car and looked up at the moon. It was a fairly new moon and it hung on the line of trees that covered the backside of the shore. Bill Carney, a logger in town, swore that he had seen a yeti once at Meater Lake, a big, hairy beast who chased him out of the parking lot. Zeb doubted he'd see a yeti tonight. Bill Carney had died during the summer. Zeb had read his obituary online, but it had made no mention of the yeti sighting.

He took deep breaths, filling his lungs purposefully. Quarterback of the Rumney Raiders, playing in the state championship game. He tried to breathe that in with the air. In all the disappointment about T.T., Zeb wondered if he himself hadn't been given a slice of opportunity. He would never have wished an injury on T.T., but now that it was here, he had to follow through. It was going to be a damn short season. A one-game season.

Two cars pulled in, their lights sweeping out to the lake. Zeb climbed back inside the Civic. The car started rough, but he got it going. On the way out of the parking lot, he saw the hindquarters of a moose. It had just entered the woods, probably going to the lake. Only its butt remained visible, then it, too, disappeared into the puckerbrush.

He pulled into Uncle Pushee's driveway and then veered off

for the camper where he and his mom lived. He turned off the engine and climbed out. The camper looked like the baby of the larger house beside it. A baby house. He took another breath. Then for the hell of it, he jumped up and grabbed the limb of an oak that partially separated the house from the camper. It was a big oak, one he had climbed as a kid, but now he simply hung from the branch, letting his shoulder muscles loosen, his back and legs stretching in good ways. He swung back and forth, remembering what it was like to climb up, to cling to the branch as you walked your feet up the trunk and curled one knee over the branch.

Starting quarterback, he told himself. He swung his legs up and bucked off, landing on his feet in a comfortable, solid way. He knocked the dirt from the branch off his hands and then pushed into the camper, hours closer to the game.

SUNDAY 2

1 T.T. = 3 Holloways

Make it 7.

Their option game is dead without T.T.

Coach K will think of something. He's our wildcard.

Holloway's the joker. The old maid. Something.

He can throw all right.

Zeb squatted next to the couch where he slept and stirred the wood stove back to life. The trailer was too small to accommodate a big stove—one where the ash could overnight easily and keep things toasty—so you had to tend it often. During the night, it went out if you didn't feed it. Zeb's job, because he slept in the living room only a stride away from the stove, was to keep it going.

Zeb knew by the light starting to come into the camper that it was time to get up and go about the day. Uncle Pushee would be awake back in the shop, his day already lined up. They had to paint the right quarter panel of the Smarts' Ford F-150 and finish pounding out the grillwork on a Nissan Sentra. *Sparks flying,* that's what Uncle Pushee said about a full day.

Zeb dressed in jeans and a ripped flannel shirt that he didn't mind getting dirty. He washed his face in the bathroom and brushed his teeth. He didn't look at himself in the mirror. He pulled on a black watch cap and slipped into his Carhartt jacket. The jacket felt stiff with dirt and oil and paint from the body shop. He squatted next to the fire and fed it up some more, bending and moving his arms deliberately to get the jacket loosened up. It felt good to move, he thought as he stepped outside.

It was a fine, crackling morning. A New Hampshire fall day, deer season. Most of the leaves had fallen, but the massive beech right behind Uncle Pushee's house still held a belfry of brown leaves that swung back and forth in the soft light. Zeb saw the deer chain—a quarter-inch chain that looped over a shank of two-by-six jammed between two small maples—had a fuzz of dried blood on its bottom end. That meant Uncle Pushee had scored a deer sometime the day before and hung it to bleed out. He would be in a good mood, Zeb figured, as he usually was when he had a hundred pounds of venison slabbed into butcher paper and stacked like white bricks in the downstairs freezer. Uncle Pushee liked to be prepared for *want or famine,* as he said.

Zeb entered the Quonset hut as the squeal of a pneumatic drill hit a high note. Uncle Pushee had something on the worktable, a flood of light bathing it.

Zeb approached and then stopped. You didn't walk up on a man while he worked with tools. That was basic shop law. You didn't want to surprise him or scare him into a sudden movement.

Zeb stood and waited for Uncle Pushee to sense him. When he did, he swung his welding helmet off and smiled. His two teeth on the bottom left had gone long ago, and when he smiled, his cheek sucked in a little on that side and made a curl in his lip. He had a frost of whiskers on his cheeks and jawline, and a thick pair of glasses that constantly slid down on his nose as if they were plotting an escape. His hands had calluses thick enough that he could snuff out a candle by lowering his palm onto it without feeling a thing. He was hard core, just as Hawny had said. *Homebrewed,* that's what other people said. He wore a brown coverall that was so filthy it could have stood up on its own if Uncle Pushee stepped out of it.

"Well, didn't you just miss some beauty of a bang last night?" Uncle Pushee started right in. "I mean to say."

"Big one?"

"One hundred and eighty-seven pounds. Belly full of acorns. Not a mark on him until we sent him out of this world. I didn't think a buck like that still existed in this day. We got him up at the Pritchetts', out by that wash of apple trees they have down that way. Waited till evening and that buck came tiptoeing out like he was keeping a date with us. Easy as picking daisies, believe me."

"You go with Whoopie?"

Uncle Pushee nodded. Whoopie was Cooper Seasons, Uncle Pushee's best friend. They had been hunting together since they were boys. Whoopie logged and cut firewood. Together, Whoopie and Uncle Pushee knew just about every game trail and fallow orchard for twenty miles around. Whoopie kept a Havahart trap baited by his bird feeder and ate gray squirrel in stews of his own devising. If an atomic bomb went off someday, Zeb knew Uncle

Pushee and Whoopie would take it right in stride. They wouldn't bat an eye.

"You still thinking of going up to deer camp?" Zeb asked, wondering if the kill the night before had changed anything.

"Why, of course I am. A man needs his rest and relaxation."

"Hawny thought he might come along."

"The more, the merrier. Whoopie might come later. We might as well bring up some of this venison. It won't get finer."

"I could ask Mom to prepare it."

Uncle Pushee smiled. Uncle Pushee had opinions about his mother, Zeb knew. Strictly speaking, she wasn't his concern. She had been married to his brother, but when his brother disappeared, Uncle Pushee let them stay on. They paid electric and ran a hose to the house. *It was complicated as a duck blind,* Zeb's mother always said. Uncle Pushee had his ways, and having a woman in his kitchen slicing up venison wasn't his way at all.

"We'll manage," Uncle Pushee said. "Let's do a bit of a cleanup around here, then we can get going on the paint job. We can leave the Sentra for another day. I have a mind to go hunting. It feels like I'm rolling sevens."

"Okay."

Uncle Pushee stuck his welding helmet back on his head. Zeb crossed the work floor and grabbed the large push broom. He pushed around the workbench, then kept brushing out to get the corners. He was still pushing and swirling when Mr. Television came in through the cat door Uncle Pushee had sawed into the workshop entrance years ago. Mr. Television was the third shop cat Zeb could remember. He was a big tortoise tom with a right ear half chewed away.

Zeb squatted down and rubbed Mr. Television's chin. The cat accepted the affection, then turned to have Zeb's hand on his body, then his butt. Zeb petted him and liked the sizzling energy that came off his hand against Mr. Television's fur.

"Feed that stupid thing, will you, when you have a chance?" Uncle Pushee called from the workbench. "Cat is going to eat me out of house and home."

"Won't it ruin his appetite for hunting if you feed him?"

Uncle Pushee touched his temple with his forefinger.

"Just do what you're told, sonny boy. Yours is not to reason why, yours is but to do or die."

"Yes, sir."

"Put a shake in it. I'm rolling sevens, Zeb. It's been a long time coming, but I'm rolling them at last."

Zeb sat with his back against the Vigil Oak, his .30-06 across his lap. Uncle Pushee had given the tree its name when he himself had hunted here as a boy. It was an enormous tree, wide as a man is tall to the breastbone, and it provided a perfect place to sit and wait for deer. A game trail cut the ridge maybe forty yards in front of it, and on a clear day with good conditions, a hunter could count on at least a handful of deer passing by. Whoopie said it was like shooting ducks at a carnival stand, but Zeb had been leaning against the tree for two hours and hadn't seen a thing. Now that night had started to pry up the darkness from the land beneath them, Zeb figured he had struck out.

He didn't know for sure, though, because he hadn't fixed his attention on hunting the way Uncle Pushee would have wanted him to. At least a dozen times he had pulled out the newspaper article Hawny had brought with him up to Dummer and read it in the gloaming. Hawny's father had cut it from the *Union Leader* and sent it along with a note at the bottom that said, *Don't grow out of your hat size.* The article was a large, splashy write-up on the sports page outlining the various divisional tournaments to be played the following weekend, and, to his astonishment, Zeb had discovered his picture dead center among the columns. Underneath the picture it said: *Senior Zeb Holloway will start for his first time in the Division 3 State Championship game in place of the injured T.T. Monroe.* The picture had been cropped from a photo taken at the start of the season. He and T.T. had posed side by side for a schoolboy preview in late August, and now the picture had reemerged and featured him as a confident-looking quarterback smiling into the camera. The article didn't have much to say about him, except to note—again—that it was his first varsity start. The writer picked the Rumney Raiders as seven-point underdogs to the Merrymeeting Mavericks. The game, the writer said, was essentially a "pick-'em," but the injury to T.T. Monroe had changed the balance of power.

Zeb patted his pocket to make sure he still had the article, then pushed up slowly from the tree. His legs and butt felt numb and cold. It was common lore that a hunter often spotted a deer the minute he stopped looking, but on this night, the deer had gone somewhere else. He stood for a second taking in the scent of the forest. By nose alone he could have returned to the cabin. He smelled the wood stove throwing out smoke and he smelled Clabbard Brook, down below the ridge where he sat, running over its bony bed to the east and south. A late chickadee made a rasping, curious chittering at his movement, and it took him a moment to realize the bird was not calling to warn about him but about Hawny, who appeared from the west, his face glowing red with cold.

"Not a thing. You?" Hawny called. "Don't shoot me, you whiz-bang."

"I'm not shooting anything. Been sitting on my duff, that's all."

"I can smell that stew from here. Let's go. I got to warm up."

"Uncle Pushee won't believe we didn't see anything."

"Uncle Pushee can bite my rump. I had my eyes peeled from that tree stand. I saw seventeen squirrels—that's it. There were some moose tracks around there, though."

Hawny stepped next to the Vigil Oak, his breath curling in front of him. He walked quietly in the woods, Zeb knew, as quiet as any person could. He smelled of liniment and cough drops, which would not please Uncle Pushee. Uncle Pushee didn't like competing smells on a deer hunter. He himself wore a sachet of deer urine around his neck when he went out dead serious for a buck. He banged antlers together too, and made other sounds to call the deer to him. Uncle Pushee had a lot of pride when it came to deer hunting.

"You ought to tell him about the game," Hawny said as they began to walk back to the cabin. "Just let him know, is all."

"He doesn't care about football."

"But he cares about you. That's the thing. He might surprise you. This is a big deal, this game."

"Not in his world, it's not."

"Well, still," Hawny said.

"He doesn't care about sports. He never thought it was a good idea for me to play in the first place. Mom supported it more than he did. She's the one who drove me to practices."

It wasn't even ten minutes back to deer camp. Whoopie's truck stood beside Uncle Pushee's. They both drove Dodge Rams and swore by them. Neither truck could be identified by its original color. Both had been parted and painted ten times or more, the reassembling taking place over much cursing and laughter in Uncle Pushee's shop. Zeb thought about how Whoopie and Uncle Pushee weren't much different from Hawny and him. They had been friends forever and that's just the way it was.

Hawny rang the small triangle on the porch to announce their arrival—you didn't simply walk into a cabin of men with rifles—then pushed through the door into the glorious warmth. As soon as Zeb moved inside, something snapped against his cheek. He heard Whoopie laugh a short bark, then Uncle Pushee joined him. Something else flew at Hawny and he dodged back, almost falling into Zeb's arms. Whoopie had a Nerf dart gun of some sort, and the orange missiles kept flying at them. Whoopie sat in his Canadian glider, a can of beer balanced between his legs. He had the Nerf rifle held out in front of him like a dousing rod stuttering in his hands.

"How many?" Uncle Pushee said, tilting his can of Pabst back in time to a rearward lean of his rocker. "Do any good?"

"Didn't see a thing," Zeb said, swatting at one more dart from Whoopie. The dart went up into the air and twirled harmlessly to the floor. Now that Zeb had seen the Nerf gun, the darts no longer presented a threat. It was like Whoopie to play a joke, Zeb reflected. It was also like Whoopie not to understand when a joke was over.

"How about you, Hawny boy?" Whoopie asked. "How many'd you get?"

"Seventeen," Hawny said.

Whoopie laughed hard at that. He looked, when he laughed, like a man on the edge of a scream. He wore a green plaid flannel overshirt tucked into tan Dickies and tall rubber boots. He had lost the top half of his right ear when a chainsaw jumped from a knot in a piece of rock maple and creased his skull. The half ear, Zeb couldn't help thinking, reminded him of a wing. It was the same ear Mr. Television had.

"While you boys are still standing, why don't you make yourselves useful and grab us a few beers?" Uncle Pushee said. "You know where to find them."

"Yes, sir."

Zeb handed Hawny his rifle. Hawny took both his and Zeb's to the small couch to the east side of the cabin to unload. Zeb stepped outside and fished two cans of Pabst from the thirty-rack beside the door. He missed being outside, he realized. He missed the quiet and the cold. He stepped back in and shut the door behind him. He passed the beers to the men. They both popped the tops at almost the same instant.

"That stew is some good," Uncle Pushee said, rocking back to nod his chin in the direction of the range. "You should get some inside you."

"Did you make biscuits to go with it?" Hawny asked, shucking the rounds out. "I think I smell biscuits."

"I wouldn't let you down, Hawny boy," Uncle Pushee said. "Finest kind too. This walrus next to me was like to eat all of them. I had to put them back in the oven before he could get to them. The butter's out on the porch to keep it cold. Out in the cooler."

Zeb went over and stood next to the stove.

"Rumor has it you're going to be playing quarterback for the Rumney Raiders," Whoopie said, drinking from his beer again. "Did I hear that correctly? That's the gossip in town."

"Looks like it," Zeb answered.

"Where did you hear that?" Uncle Pushee asked Whoopie.

"Down at the Burning Bush. I was picking up that come-along that I needed."

"What did they get you for it?"

"Sixty-two eighty. But it's a good rig. I couldn't make do with a Walmart special. I've got heavy equipment."

"Of course you do," Uncle Pushee agreed.

"He's going to start in a state championship game," Hawny said from the couch. "Saturday over at the UNH field. Old Zebulon here. How about that?"

Uncle Pushee rocked and drank his beer. Whoopie drank too, but he brought his mouth off the can to ask another question.

"Isn't that what I heard exactly?" Whoopie asked. "They were talking about it to beat the band. Lyle, that one, and his Saturday help . . . what's his name?"

"Kevin Ball," Uncle Pushee said. "He's Steven's kid."

"Anyway, he was saying that Junior here is going to be playing a big old game next Saturday. They said you're replacing one heck of a quarterback. A black kid."

"T.T. Monroe," Hawny said. "But Zeb's going to make it rain

out there! He can throw better than T.T. ever could. Zeb's going to light it up, just wait and see."

"What time will you be back?" Uncle Pushee asked. "Will you make it on Sunday morning?"

"Yes, sir."

"Maybe we should just take a run down there and watch this game," Whoopie said.

"You *should* come," Hawny said, leaning the rifles up against the wall and coming to the stove. "It's not like he's going to go play for the Patriots after this. I mean, this is his last stand, football-wise."

"Last game," Uncle Pushee acknowledged, dropping his head so his chin bounced against his chest. "Hang 'em up after this, right?"

"He could be the winning quarterback for the state championship game, Uncle Pushee," Hawny said, backing his butt closer to the stove. "He's in the *Union Leader* today."

"You don't say?" Whoopie said and raised his eyebrows. "We're hunting with a celebrity! If I'da known that, I'da worn better clothes."

"The *Union Mis-Leader*?" Uncle Pushee asked, smiling at Whoopie.

"You've been in there a couple times, Pushee. In the police log!"

That went over big. Zeb moved through the chairs and snagged two bowls off the makeshift kitchen counter. He tossed one to Hawny and Hawny caught it easily. Hawny slipped on a welder's glove and lifted the lid from the pan of stew. Zeb grabbed four biscuits out of the gas oven. He carried them over to the stove and handed Hawny two. Hawny held the lid up for him while he ladled two big splashes of stew into his bowl.

"Growing boys," Whoopie said. "Make your supper. Old Pushee here has more deer than John Deere! Eat up! We're eating like kings, boys. Nothing finer!"

The stew was tasty. Zeb discovered his hunger even as he ate. He felt restless and uneasy, but he couldn't name the cause. The game pressed on him. It was one thing to be told you were going to play in the most important game of the season, another thing entirely to do it. He didn't feel confident. He wondered if he hadn't been fooling himself all along. He had no business leading the Rumney team into the state championship. Everyone knew it, but no one could say it aloud. It felt like hearing a joke and watching people around you laugh but not getting the punch line no matter which way you turned it.

Uncle Pushee and Whoopie began a long argument about the price of the come-along. Uncle Pushee kept asking if the device had been made in America. Whoopie contended that made no difference at all. Uncle Pushee said that anything that had to cross water ended up being more expensive. That was just the way of things, he said. It was stupid to think otherwise.

"You want to ride back tonight?" Zeb asked Hawny when they finished eating.

He cleaned the bowls left in the sink. Hawny sat on the counter beside him, his heels occasionally tapping the structure underneath. Zeb smelled cold and autumn on Hawny. He wondered if he smelled that way himself.

"I thought we were going to sleep over. Maybe take a try for a deer in the morning."

"If I'm late to school, I can't practice. If I can't practice, I can't play on Saturday."

"That sucks. I want to go after one in the morning. We could leave here by eight or nine."

"I'd be late."

Hawny nodded. After other weekends, they could come into school sometime before noon and no one much bothered about it. Zeb knew this week was different. He didn't dare chance it. Coach K had said something about leadership. You didn't demonstrate leadership by showing up to school late. He hoped Hawny understood that.

"We can go, I guess," Hawny said. "Leave these two up here to spoon and keep each other warm."

Hawny said that loud enough so Whoopie would overhear. Whoopie turned and fired Nerf darts at Hawny. Hawny blocked them like a tiny bear swatting at bees. Zeb finished washing out the bowls and stacking them to dry in the dish drainer. A dart hit his shoulder blade as he hung up the dishtowel.

"We're thinking about heading back home," Zeb said. "I can't be late for school tomorrow."

"You don't want to take a run at them in the morning?" Uncle Pushee asked. "It's funny we didn't see any tonight."

He had risen from his chair and ducked outside to pee and grab more beer. Now as he settled back in, he swiveled the chair a little to see them better behind him.

"Oh, those deer have been pretty picked over," Whoopie said, taking the darts that Hawny gathered for him. "They get the message, believe me. They know not to show themselves for another two weeks."

"They've still got to eat, just like every other creature on earth. They have to come out sometime."

"I should get back," Zeb said, trying to stay focused. "Just this one time."

"Be a dark road out there," Uncle Pushee said. "Mind the moose."

"Can't see the blessed things until they're on top of you," Whoopie said. "Like driving into a walking tree."

"We'll take it easy," Zeb said. "Won't we, Hawny?"

"Heck no!"

Part of his wanting to leave, Zeb knew, was simply to be outside again. It felt too warm in the cabin, too close all the way around. He wanted to be back out under the stars. He thought a ring of his body—like a tree ring—might die if he didn't get outside. Sometimes the stars got into his blood. He didn't know why they did, but he knew it was true.

It took ten minutes to pack up. They chucked their things in the back of Hawny's truck. The moon had continued on its journey and gone below the horizon. A tree rubbed somewhere against another tree when the wind shuffled things around. Hawny started the truck to get it warming.

"Thanks, Uncle Pushee," Zeb said, bringing two more beers to the men as a gift of departure. "See you back at the place. Sorry we got skunked."

"I may stay till noon or so tomorrow."

"You want me to put up a sign on the shop?"

"Yeah, maybe you should. Just say I'll be back midafternoon."

"Yes, sir."

They didn't shake hands. They hardly ever shook hands, Zeb

realized. Whoopie began peppering them with Nerf darts on the way out the door. Zeb threw one back at Whoopie and it fluttered into the old man's lap. He ducked outside before taking another volley, and the air punched him in the chest with a bright blue yearning. He drew a breath until it filled him. He reached down and picked up a stone and threw it at the trunk of the old clothesline pine. The stone snapped dead center into the bole of the tree.

Mr. Television sat on the step of the shop. Zeb bent down to pet him as Hawny pulled back down the driveway, his horn blaring "La Cucaracha" as he hit the street. Lights shone from the camper, which meant his mother was home. Arthur's car stood next to his mother's Honda Civic. Arthur drove a Toyota Corolla, the world's most boring car. Zeb rubbed Mr. Television's chin. The cat probably needed food. He was always hungry.

Zeb turned on the workbench light inside the shop and wrote out a sign in marker that said Uncle Pushee would be back in the midafternoon on Monday. It took him a few minutes to find Scotch tape and he almost tripped over Mr. Television as he searched. Mr. Television wound himself around Zeb's feet, asking for food the only way he knew how.

Zeb posted the sign and carried the marker back to the workbench. When he put the marker in the top drawer, he traded it for a black-and-white photo of Lawrence Pushee, his father. The picture was not a surprise to him; he checked it whenever he found himself alone in the workshop. Zeb couldn't say whether Uncle Pushee knew the picture existed, but he certainly never referenced it. It seemed no different, really, than the odd washers and bolts and carpenter pencils scattered haphazardly across the workbench. It was something old and obsolete, something that belonged to a forgotten project, yet it was not quite worth throwing away. It was almost as if Uncle Pushee might someday have a use for such a thing, so he didn't bother carrying it to the plastic bin that they used for everything else they couldn't burn in the shop wood stove. They were half brothers, Lawrence and Uncle Pushee. Same mother, different fathers.

Zeb bent to examine the photo more closely under the fluorescent shop light. It was a good photo. It was a photo that had some artistic value, Zeb thought, even if his dad hadn't been the subject. It captured Lawrence Pushee as he vaulted a plank fence, probably somewhere in his early twenties. He looked thin and long, and his hair, shaggy and down to his shoulders, flew backward in the leap. His face had a funny smile tucked down by his chin, and his eyes, Lawrence's eyes, revealed amusement at whoever snapped the photo.

Zeb had looked at it a thousand times and had only noted the dog—a spotted brown dog, maybe knee height, its front quarters squeezing under the bottom rung of the fence—after a couple dozen viewings. The dog presented a puzzle, a pleasant puzzle, and Zeb liked wondering at their relationship. Was it his father's dog? If so, what was its name? Zeb tried to see his own face in his father's face, but his father's glance was too downward to make a fair evaluation. Still, something in his dad's movement, the length of his forearm in proportion to his biceps, struck Zeb as familiar.

Zeb ran his thumb over the photograph and put it back where he had found it. Where he always found it. He filled Mr. Television's bowl with kibble, then turned out the shop lights and crossed the yard to the camper. He found Arthur standing in the doorway, his coat halfway up his right arm, his mom helping him with the other. Arthur smelled of whiskey and of flimsy lavender cologne. His hair—a reddish comb-over—had lifted from his head to give him a halo that danced on top of his scalp as he tried to get his right arm all the way in his jacket. The awkwardness of his attempt made his mother laugh.

"Oh, you're home, Zebby. Arthur was just leaving. I thought you were sleeping out at deer camp?" his mother said when he stepped inside, passing close to Arthur. He had tried to give them time to get organized before he came to the door.

"Hi, Arthur," Zeb said. "How you doing?"

"I'd be doing fine if I could get this damn coat on. I'll tell you that much. I'm like a darn dog chasing its tail."

Zeb went to the couch and began making up his bed. He hoped if he didn't engage them too much, the night would end easily, but suddenly Arthur had his hand out.

"It's great news about the game," Arthur said. "About the state championship . . . and you playing. That's really terrific."

It required a moment for Zeb to understand Arthur wanted to shake hands. It felt peculiar to shake the man's hand in his own house, a man he had known for quite a while.

"Well, thanks."

"It's big. It's really a big thing."

"Well, it seems to be growing, that's for sure."

Arthur didn't let go of his hand. Not for three or four more shakes than they needed. Zeb realized, standing next to him, that he was taller than Arthur now. Arthur no longer felt big to him.

"We're proud of our boy," Zeb's mom said. "He was in the paper. Zeb, everyone's been calling about it! You should have said something."

"I didn't know I was going to be in it. I would have said something, but I didn't know."

Arthur finally dropped his hand. The camper was too small for all of them to be moving around like this. Arthur wasn't finished, though.

"Our team was in the semifinals one year. I guess you could call it that. I didn't get in the game and we lost anyway. We lost to Calvert Hall, a Catholic school from over by Keene."

"Oh, Arthur," Zeb's mom said from behind the man. "Zeb doesn't need your old war stories. He needs to get to bed. Now, scoot. Did you get a deer, honey?"

Zeb shook his head.

"How about Uncle Pushee or Whoopie?"

"Why's he called Whoopie anyway?" Arthur asked, his movement a beat too slow. He turned to face Zeb's mom, obviously trying to be sociable.

"Oh, I don't know," she said. "Some crazy reason."

"Well, it's going to be a big day on Saturday."

"Yes, sir."

Arthur left. Zeb went to the bathroom and washed up, then came out and filled the wood stove. He tried to read a few pages for English. He was supposed to be reading *Gulliver's Travels,* but he didn't much like it. It felt slow and tedious. In between the words, he listened to his mother saying good night to Arthur. Sometimes they made no noise and he knew they were kissing. When she came back in, he had his book back in front of his nose.

"I'm mad at you, Zebulon," she said, pushing his feet up so she could sit near the stove. "Mad that you didn't tell me! I shouldn't have to find out something like that from someone else. From the general public!"

"Mom," he said, lowering his book. "Drop it, okay?"

"I will not drop it. I was embarrassed when Arthur told me. I can't keep track of your football career on top of everything else, can I?"

"Of course not, Mom."

"Now, I'm going to try everything I can think of to get off Saturday, but you know how it is. That's the day after Black Friday, one of the biggest shopping days of the year. The biggest day, I guess. I don't know what Lorelei will say. She's a friend, but she's also the manager. She has to have shifts covered."

"It's okay, Mom."

"I want to see you play, Zeb, honey. But bills are still bills."

He put his book up in front of him. He knew Mrs. Scattergood would quiz them tomorrow. She said she refused to stand up in front of a class and try to discuss a book that no one had read. He didn't exactly blame her, but that didn't make *Gulliver's Travels* any more exciting.

"I love you, honey, and I'm very proud of you. Everyone around you is proud of you. I hope you know that."

"I know, Mom. Thanks."

"Even Arthur in his way . . . he was really quite complimentary about you. Very impressed."

"Okay, Mom."

He felt sleep coming over him. He thought of the stars again and the scent of the woods deep in the frost. The world was a pretty place. When his mom got up and moved back to her room, he jolted awake for a second. He thought she was a deer for a fraction of an instant, and then he remembered where he was, and the light from the wood stove made yellow ghosts on the ceiling.

MONDAY 3

"T.T.'s leaving," Stella said, her face flushed and red. "He's going to a hospital in Texas and he's staying there afterward."

"In the hospital?"

"No, doofus. In Texas. He's moving to Texas."

Zeb regarded her carefully. Rain hit against the window of the cafeteria. It was sixth period, second block, a forty-five-minute study hall. The study-hall supervisor, Mrs. Catalonia, didn't care if you talked as long as you kept it quiet. Zeb always sat with Stella. They always talked.

He studied her face, trying to determine what the news meant to her. At the same time, he wasn't sure what it meant to him. He always felt a little clueless and confused when he sat near Stella. Today, especially, she distracted him. She wore a navy sweater and a bunch of thin gold chains that made up some kind of necklace. Whenever she moved or leaned forward, the chains swung out and away. The entire apparatus of being female—the chains, the bright, silvery studs in her ears, the gloss on her lips, the hint of perfume that accompanied all her movements, the roundness of her breasts beneath the sweater—interested him and confounded him in the same breath. He wanted to reach across the cafeteria table and take her hand, although he wasn't quite sure why. He wanted to touch her, but the best he could do for the moment was nod his head and let his eyes climb into hers.

"Why is he going?" he managed finally.

"They want to take him to a specialist. I guess he's going to a doctor who operates on the Dallas Cowboys. A sports medicine specialist. It just seems crazy to me. They're trying to hurry it, because it doesn't do any good to delay. Every day is a loss for his potential recovery. That's what they say."

"They don't trust the doctors here?"

"Something like that," she said. "I don't really know. We're not getting along right now."

"Sorry."

"Are you?" she asked, smiling.

Her smile killed him. It was the wrong kind of smile to give to someone who was just a friend. She flirted, but he knew she flirted with everyone. The smile didn't make him feel special.

"Anyway," she continued, "he's going to finish school out there. His dad is military and he's being reposted in Texas. Something about a security team. I don't understand it all. It makes sense to have him seen by a doctor where they will be living, I suppose. I don't know."

"I don't blame them. He's good enough that you want the best doctors. I mean, he's really that good."

"I know. I know. Everyone says so."

"You don't think he is?"

"I liked T.T. for what he was. For what he is. He can be sweet. As sweet as anything. Being a football player is only part of who he is, but it's the most important part."

"When does he leave?"

"Today, maybe. Maybe tomorrow."

"He's going to miss the game."

She shrugged.

"T.T.'s more about himself than he is about the team," she said. "You know that. Everyone knows that."

"Still."

"He cares, it's just he sees himself as bigger than the team. This injury has really turned him upside down. Suddenly his whole identity is in question. He saw his life going in a certain direction, and now it isn't necessarily going that way. It's thrown him for a loop. You can understand that."

"I guess so. I can see that."

"You're not like him that way. Football is just a small part of your life. You know it's just a game."

"Maybe that's because I'm not as good as T.T."

"Maybe. Or maybe you have better things to think about."

She smiled again. This time she made a funny face.

Rain continued to hit against the windowpane. A kid on the freshman team named Buzzer walked by and held out his hand for a knuckle-bump. Zeb knuckle-bumped him and nodded. That kind of thing had been happening all day. People who he hardly knew suddenly talked to him or knuckle-bumped him. It had to do with being quarterback for the state championship game, that was all. He knew a week from now, all of that would fade, especially if it didn't go well. It was even possible things would turn against him if he played poorly.

He turned his attention back to Stella, but she had a copy of *Vogue* open in front of her and she licked her finger when she turned the page. He felt their conversation still had territory to cover, but the news about T.T.'s departure hadn't settled inside him. Part of him thought T.T. was being something of a jerk not to stay around for the state championship game, but another part realized T.T. had to look after his own interests. He could have a future in the game, whereas the championship, win or lose, was the end of the road for almost every other player on the team.

He was still thinking of a way to reopen the conversation with Stella when Buzzer and another ninth-grader walked over.

"Coach K wants to see you," the kid said, stopping to hand Zeb a hall pass. Zeb took it and examined it. "He's down at the gym in his office."

"Now?"

The kid nodded. Buzzer leaned his shoulder into the kid's shoulder to knock him sideways. Stella looked up when one of the chairs scooted slightly to one side. Zeb glanced quickly to see if Mrs. Catalonia had heard. If she had, she didn't bother tracking down the sound.

"Tell him I'll be right there," Zeb told the kid. "What's your name anyway?"

"Patrick."

"You're not on the team, are you?"

"Not this year."

“Not any freaking year!” Buzzer laughed. “His mommy won’t let him play. She’s afraid he’ll scramble his brains.”

“I don’t blame her,” Stella said, looking up. “It’s a primitive game played by apes.”

Buzzer scratched under his armpits like a monkey. Zeb smiled. Buzzer could be pretty funny sometimes. Truth was, Zeb agreed with Stella for the most part. It was a brutal, absurd game, but he loved it anyway.

“Okay, I’ll go find Coach in a minute,” he told the two underclassmen. “Thanks.”

“Coach K snaps his fingers and everyone runs,” Stella said. “I won’t miss that.”

“You mean with T.T. gone?”

“I mean this whole school. I mean everyone being so wrapped up in it. It’s all anyone talks about. Did you see the banners they put up downtown? They’re everywhere. All the shop windows have these handmade signs saying *Beat Merrymeeting.*”

“Isn’t it nice that the town supports the team?”

“It’s nice, but don’t the adults have anything else to think about?”

She held up the magazine.

“If you had to date one girl on this page, who would it be?”

“The girl on the right.”

“Her? She looks skanky. Why do you like her?”

“I don’t know. She looks nice.”

“Do you think she’s hot?”

“I don’t know. You asked, so I picked one.”

Zeb began collecting his books. He didn’t have many. He slid

Gulliver's Travels on top. He put Coach K's hall pass in the center of the novel.

"I should go," he said.

"I didn't mean I'm not happy for you. For the chance you're getting," she said. "T.T. says you'll do fine. And it is a big deal."

"Thanks."

"And I'll cheer for you. Rah, rah, rah."

Her nose crinkled again. He wished, somehow, he could stop things and tell her how those two minuscule dents on either side of her nose completely slayed him. The thought of saying something like that sounded crazy even to him. He stood.

"Why do you cheer if you don't like it?"

"It's what people do in high school, Zeb. It's something to do."

She stuck out her bottom lip. Then she reached over and grabbed his hand. She wrote *Go Raiders!* on his forearm in pink marker. Mrs. Catalonia called to him to see what he was doing. Students were not allowed to move around in study hall. He held up the hall pass and answered that Coach K wanted to see him. He brought the pass up to Mrs. Catalonia. She signed the bottom. People watched him as he walked out. That had been happening all day too. He turned at the door to see if Stella watched, but she had her nose back in her magazine, the rainy window framing her in pearl gray.

T.T. ran a 4.3 forty.

Bull.

He did. He signed for USC. USC doesn't sign slow people.

Holloway is about half as fast as T.T.

Holloway is not a runner. What don't you get about that?

Merrymeeting looks great. The d end is massive.

In Coach K we trust. Trust in Coach K, brother.

Coach K sat in his school office beside the boys' locker room. It was a different office from the one upstairs in the field house, which was really a communal space for trainers and boosters and film sessions. Coach K, Zeb knew, taught two sections of phys ed, one of geometry, and two blocks of drivers' ed. His real job, of course, was to coach the football team, but that didn't get talked about much as far as Zeb could tell. Every boy at the high school knew Coach K's office. It was decorated with school surplus and might have been mistaken for a storage room if a person didn't know better. A ship-metal-gray desk took up the center space and an assortment of chairs and stools ringed it. A plywood set of shelves against the back wall held a hundred trophies for teams he had coached. The trophies looked too large for the room, like imitation pirate treasure buried in a sea cave.

Zeb saw Coach K through the window before he knocked. Coach K had a film clip going. The players on the screen ran backward in front of Coach K. Then, as Zeb knocked, they started forward again. Coach K lifted his left hand and flexed his fingers: *Come in.* Zeb pushed through. The defensive backs coach, Coach Steve, sat in the darkness well away from the screen. Coach Steve was young and worked at Merrill Lynch, a stock brokerage, all day until practice. His suits were better than any of the other coaches' suits. Coach Steve had played safety at Kutztown State.

"Come on in, Zeb," Coach K said, his voice tired and heavy. "How's your weekend?"

"Good, thanks."

"Have a seat. Coach Steve, will you give us a minute? I want to take a minute with Zeb here."

"No problem," Coach Steve said, lifting himself to his feet. "I need to go get changed anyway."

Zeb sat. Coach K watched the video for another play, then froze it. Coach K was famous for his ability to dissect film, Zeb knew. People said if he had sufficient time to study another team, the other team was doomed. Zeb didn't know if that was true, but he certainly hoped so.

"So I don't know how much you've heard or haven't heard," Coach K began, reaching to his necktie and pulling it away from his throat. Coach K seldom wore a tie and he looked uncomfortable in it. He yanked it slowly back and forth, moving it down his chest like someone swinging the clapper of a bell. "But T.T. is taking off for Texas. He's got a medical opinion there . . . a team of doctors. I guess his family feels he can get better care in Dallas. His folks came from down that way, San Antonio, I believe. Anyway, that's the long and the short of it."

"Yes, sir."

"He won't be at the game. It's important he gets his leg situation addressed as soon as possible."

"Yes, sir."

"Which brings us to you."

Zeb waited. He felt his skin blanch. He leaned forward slightly to hear the coach better, at the same time becoming aware that he had trouble focusing on Coach K's face. Coach K looked directly into Zeb's eyes and Zeb had to exert all his concentration to keep from looking away. The players on the screen beside Coach K remained locked in stillness.

"We're thinking of giving Dello Russo a shot at quarterback," Coach K said. "You know Jimbo. He's a bit flaky sometimes, but he's a good athlete. He's a lefty and lefties can be a little wild, but he can run. He runs well, as you know."

Zeb nodded. He could not control the blood that moved around his body.

"This is not a demotion. And I'm not sure who I'm going to start on Saturday, but I wanted you to hear it from me first. Do you have any questions?"

"I thought I performed pretty well last week."

"You did. You did fine. This is no reflection on that, believe me. Merrymeeting presents certain defensive sets that might cause us problems, especially if we lose our running game at quarterback. It's possible we'll platoon you and Jimbo. It's also possible we won't play him at all. T.T.'s injury took us all by surprise. I'm sure you can understand that."

Zeb nodded. He couldn't trust himself to speak more than he had.

"I've already talked to Jimbo. We're going to try a few things in practice and see how it goes. Are you okay with this, son?"

Zeb nodded again.

"Let's have a good week of practice. I want you to be watching film with Coach Hoch. Jimbo will sit in. We have Alan as a third backup, but he's a sophomore and probably won't make a difference one way or the other. This is all about the next man up. Who's going to take us to the state championship?"

Zeb thought for a horrible moment that he might be sick. He thought he might throw up right on the coach's desk. He squared his shoulders and tried to compose himself. Something vaguely unfair had just happened, but he couldn't bring it to the front of his mind. Jimbo wasn't a quarterback. He was a wild, athletic kid who threw javelin for the track team every spring. He had a huge arm, but he wasn't a quarterback.

"Is that all, Coach?" he managed to say.

"We want you to keep your attitude up. As I said, this isn't a demotion. We want to make sure we have options. Do you hear what I'm saying?"

Zeb nodded.

"It's all about different tools," Coach K said, finally sliding his tie off from around his neck. "We all bring different tools to the game. The main thing is to win next Saturday."

Zeb stood. A reckless thought passed through his head: *Screw it.* He could walk out right now and be done with it all. What had been something clean and beautiful, a chance to do something worthwhile and important for the team and for himself, had suddenly been dragged into a pile of second-guessing. He looked for a moment at Coach K and for the first time since Zeb had known the coach, his eyes defeated the eyes of the older man. That was something remarkable. Deep down, Coach K couldn't touch him. That was a thing Zeb hadn't known before. Zeb stood there for a second wondering what to do about this new understanding.

"I'll see you at practice," Zeb said.

"Did you get a deer?"

How did he know about deer hunting? Coach K did not have the right to ask about deer hunting. Not after what had just passed between them. Zeb walked out without responding. When he opened the door, he nearly ran into Jimbo.

"'S'up?" Jimbo asked.

Zeb raised his chin in reply. Behind him he heard Coach K call to Jimbo to step inside.

"America's infatuation with football is America's infatuation with land, conquering land, taking from the Native Americans the fruits and comforts of the land. Europeans eradicated the bison, threw up barbed wire to section off what had always been open range, and generously repaid the red man's generosity with smallpox and gonorrhea. That's why Americans love football, don't you agree, Mr. Holloway?"

Zeb stared at Mr. Heywood. Mr. Heywood stood in front of a tepee at the side of the class, his gray hair wild, his corduroy suit coat old and too big. He wore Birkenstock sandals and carried something he called a coup stick, a painted wooden club with feathers fluttering at the end. Mr. Heywood was a popular teacher, a teacher who at least didn't bore everyone to death, and so when he asked the question, Zeb knew he was simply being provocative.

"I don't know, Mr. Heywood. I don't know why Americans love football."

"Did you know, Mr. Holloway, that the typical game of American football involves only eleven to fourteen minutes of actual play? That the majority of the time we spend watching football, we are looking at an endless parade of men lining up and walking back and forth while other men, former players, talk about what might happen next? And we eat and stay sedentary and we ruin our health. That's American football."

"And the ads," June O'Dell said from the other side of the

room. June O'Dell was tops in the class and was Mr. Heywood's personal Igor, always backing him up on any line of reasoning he decided to take.

"Yes, of course, and the ads. Football is an advertisement that says to the nation that conquering land is the goal of life. You're going to be the quarterback in the biggest game of the season, Mr. Holloway, so what do you have to say for yourself?"

Zeb didn't have anything to say for himself. Not really. He didn't think about football that way. Besides, he knew Mr. Heywood was using him for something to do in the last minutes of the school day. Mr. Heywood prided himself on not sticking to the syllabus.

"I say beat Merrymeeting," Zeb said.

That brought a laugh. Even Mr. Heywood smiled.

"Touché. But do you think the nature of football in some way or manner reflects the inner id of our national impulse toward cruelty and dominance?"

"I have no idea, Mr. Heywood," Zeb said. "That could be."

He glanced at the clock. Seven minutes remained in the school day.

"How about anyone else? We shouldn't pick on Mr. Holloway just because he is the quarterback for the team. That isn't fair. But this school is making a big deal out of a game that will take place next Saturday. What is this obsession our culture has about football?"

"It's other sports too," June O'Dell said. "It's not just football. We're sports-crazy. And look at the salaries players get paid. It's insane."

"But football is far and away the most popular sport in

America. It's no coincidence that it is perfectly suited for television. Dramatic action followed by long pauses so the nachos can be prepared."

"Nachos!" Kenny Long shouted, putting hunger and lust into the phrase. He was a heavy kid who wore vintage Black Sabbath T-shirts.

That brought a laugh too.

People began packing up their books and some pulled out their cell phones. Mr. Heywood reminded them they were supposed to read a document he had posted online, a colonial document written by a minister about one of the first Thanksgivings. Zeb put his head down on the desk for a second. He felt tired and sleepy. He thought of Coach K telling him so casually that they would work in Jimbo. It stung. But rather than making him angry, it seemed to take all his energy away.

When the bell rang, Mr. Heywood stood in front of Zeb's desk. He reached out his coup stick and touched Zeb on the shoulder.

"You cannot be a full brave until you count coup in the Crow culture. That's the appropriate answer, Mr. Holloway. When a young man touches his enemy and escapes or steals a horse, that's counting coup. You are trying to count coup on Saturday."

"If you say so, Mr. Heywood."

"I do say so. Let some thoughts in, Zeb. You have a better mind that you admit to. Don't be afraid to play with ideas."

"Yes, sir."

"Good luck in the game, Zeb. I'll be pulling for you."

"Thank you, Mr. Heywood."

Zeb stood. He couldn't shake his sleepiness. He walked to his locker and could hardly lift his hand to turn the combination.

When he opened the door, a bouquet of curled crepe paper floated up in the air, trailing the motion and wind created by the swing of the door. Someone had taped his picture—the one that had appeared in the paper—on the inside of the door. Someone had also hung from the coat hook a paper bag with the word *Treats* written across the side in gold stars and sequins. His number, number 14, was written maybe fifty times all over the bag in blue and white marker.

Zeb stood for a second, trying to make sense of it. Then he saw a small card taped above his picture and he opened it. It read: *Beat Merrymeeting. Go Zeb!* It was signed by his "little sister." Her name was Laura Hayworth. Zeb had never heard of her.

He pulled out the bag of treats and opened it. Smarties, miniature Snickers bars, Tootsie Rolls, Kit Kats, M&M's, Milk Duds, peanut butter cups, and a handful of fireballs. Zeb stepped back and looked around. He wondered how someone had gotten into his locker.

He took out a peanut butter cup and then rolled the top of the bag closed. He unwrapped the foil around it and put the candy on his tongue. It began to melt in deliciousness almost immediately. He looked around again, scanning the hallway. He wondered if Laura, whoever she was, had watched him open his locker. He wondered what he should do to thank her. When he closed his locker door, a few strands of the crepe-paper bouquet stuck out and fluttered softly in the wind created by his classmates passing by.

Zeb put one foot behind the other and bent slowly from the waist, letting his hamstring stretch in a long, even pull. It felt good to stretch. It felt good to be on the field. He didn't want to think about what Coach K had proposed about splitting the quarterback position; Zeb hadn't mentioned it to anyone, not even Hawny, who stretched beside him now. Hawny made creaky-door sounds whenever he stretched, thinking it was funny, but that was Hawny's way and he had always done it. In the past Zeb might have joined him making cracks about the exercises, but not now, not since T.T. had gone down.

Zeb switched legs, stretched that hamstring. Afterward they did ten burpees, run in place, run in place, down, up, down, up, run in place, run in place, down, up. They sprinted the last one off, and Zeb sprinted twenty yards. He wasn't fast but he ran hard, figuring he had come this far and now was not the time to let up. He never let up, not really. Whatever Coach K decided to do was his business. Zeb understood he couldn't change a thing about it. He knew he could only handle his own preparation and he committed to doing that as fully as possible.

Coach Hoch blew a long, shrill whistle. Coach K waved the boys in and told them to take a knee. Some of the kids started beating on their thigh pads. *Thump, thump, thummmmmmpppp.* Zeb knelt beside Hawny. Water from the sopping ground turned his kneecap cold. Zeb looked at a red oak behind Coach K. The leaves had all dropped away except in close to the trunk, where the wind couldn't find them. The thumping grew louder and some of the kids started yelling and whistling. Coach Steve, dressed in a Kutztown State sweatshirt, trotted among the kneeling boys and slapped their helmets or knuckle-bumped their fists. A light rain began to fall. Zeb watched a few of the boosters in the bleachers pull out umbrellas. He smelled cigar smoke from where the boosters stood.

Coach K waved his hands to tell them to simmer down. The sound cut off in pieces, like a chainsaw bratting on a hunk of frozen wood.

"Hey, hey, hey," Coach K said, grinning and looking with his fierce eyes around the semicircle of boys, "what do we have this week?"

Everything started back up. *Thump, thump, thummmmmpppp.* Coach Steve threw a bunch of punches into the air and did a ridiculous karate kick. Coach Larentino, the line coach, smiled a long, broad smile. He was the oldest of the coaches. He had gray hair cut to a landing strip on top of his head.

"State championship!" Coach Steve yelled. "Championship Saturday!"

Zeb heard some pounding and shouting from the boosters and realized those older men had joined in the ritual. He thought about the picture of his father vaulting the rail fence and thought of Uncle Pushee and Whoopie drinking PBRs up at the Dummer camp. They would never stand around watching boys get ready for a football game. They wouldn't know what to say to someone who did.

Finally, everyone settled.

"That's right, men," Coach K said, his voice low and steady. "That's what we're playing for. We're playing for a state championship. For an undefeated season. For all the marbles."

No one said anything in reply. The other coaches had reverent expressions on their faces. Zeb didn't dare glance at Hawny. Hawny, he knew, would remember whatever Coach K said and turn it into a parody later. Hawny always had a field day with sentimentality.

"You have to ask yourselves . . . each one of you . . . you have to ask yourself deep down in that place that no one else knows about, no one else can get to: Are you ready? Are you ready to give everything to your teammates? Are you ready to bust your guts out of love and dedication to this team? Don't just speak it. Mean it. If you mean it, then speak it. If you speak it, then mean it. Are you clear, men?"

A bunch of boys around Zeb nodded. He felt them quivering. Coach K had them all stirred up. The coaches behind him nodded and kept nodding even when Coach K didn't speak. Zeb knew a religious celebration when he saw one. His mother occasionally made him attend revivals in the summer at the Baptist church over in Campton. His grandmother in Maine dragged everyone to church whenever she could. He half turned to see Hawny, but then caught himself and turned back.

"Merrymeeting is a good team. They are a fine team. Make no mistake about that. They'll play hard for four quarters. Don't think they'll give up, no matter what. But Merrymeeting isn't Rumney, is it? We are the Rumney Raiders. We have history on our side. We have tradition. We have terrific players who have dedicated themselves to this team and this town. We have great coaches, super coaches, and every year other teams contact our coaches about moving away to a different town to start their own programs. They don't go. They don't go because we are the Rumney Raiders, do you understand? We are synonymous with quality and tradition. And remember, tradition never graduates."

Coach K walked slowly among the kneeling boys. He didn't speak in a rush. He paused in long, dramatic silences. He gave them laser eyes. Zeb didn't look toward the coach, but he didn't look away either. He was done with looking away from anyone.

"Saturday morning at eleven, we play for the New Hampshire state championship. They're expecting twenty thousand people to attend. That's a bigger crowd than most towns' populations. That should give you some perspective. That should give you some notion of what this game means to a whole lot of people. Now, if I have to motivate you, if I have to rev you up, then you don't have a heart. That's the plain and simple truth. If you can't feel it here," he said, pointing to his heart, "and here"—he pointed to his balls—"then there's no help for you."

Zeb would have wagered a million dollars that Hawny was already working on a routine about Coach touching his balls. It was too perfect to ignore. Zeb was about to turn to check with Hawny when he felt the coach suddenly lift him by the shoulder pads. Before he knew it, he found himself on his feet beside Coach K. Coach K put his arm around Zeb's shoulders.

"We can't pretend that T.T. leaving isn't a loss. It's a huge loss. Zeb knows it. That's no secret to anyone here. What is a secret, a secret even from Merrymeeting, is that we have a fine backup quarterback. Zeb is going to play a whale of a game. I can feel it. I bet you can too. And we're going to spend some time working in Jimbo, too, for some running game and a few other novelty plays. We're going to do whatever it takes to put points on the board. Do you all hear me? Are you going to rally around Zeb and Jimbo and help them help us win states?"

Everyone cheered. Zeb felt absurd standing beside the coach. Coach Hoch, who had arrived late from talking with one of the boosters, grabbed Jimbo and made him stand too. The team pounded their thigh pads. One of the boosters honked an air horn. Then Coach K quieted them just enough to ask for a good week of practice. He said to put all distractions behind them for one week of their lives. He said they wouldn't regret it.

"Do you want to be state champs or not?" Coach K said.

"Yes," the team answered.

"Are you going to give it everything?"

"Yes."

"Is it your choice to be a champion?"

"Yes."

"Then break into squads and let's have a great practice!"

That was it. Zeb turned and trotted toward the grandstand where the backs usually assembled. It felt strange to gather without T.T.; T.T. was a magnet, no question, and now that he was missing, the rest of the backs felt scattered and unsure. Zeb broke apart and grabbed some footballs. A quarterback always had to have footballs. That was job number one. He picked up four and booted a fifth one in the general direction of the group of backs. The ball went up and caught the light from the grandstands on its sides. When it came down, it looked like part of the sky had broken loose and was falling recklessly to earth. No one looked up to dodge away or mark its passing.

"Would you say you feel it more here? Or here?" Hawny asked for the thousandth time since they had left practice, pointing first to his heart, then to his balls. "I personally feel it in both, but I much prefer my balls."

"Give it up, Hawny."

"The man is insane, I tell you. Coach K, all the way! He's crazy. He's always been crazy."

"He's just trying to get us revved up for Saturday."

"I know that. I know what's he's doing. How about this Jimbo business? When did that happen?"

"He called me down before last period to tell me. I don't blame him, really. It's just to give some running balance to the offense."

"It depends on whether he feels it here"—Hawny pointed to his heart—"or here." To his balls.

Despite everything, Zeb felt good. Practice had gone okay. The offense had responded well to his leadership. They seemed crisp. Even Coach Hoch said so. Now sitting in Hawny's jacked-up truck, the heat blasting, his hair sometimes dripping a shivery vein of cold shower water onto his shoulders, he felt all right. True, Jimbo had taken some reps, but not many. Clearly they saw Jimbo as an emergency backup, a difficult match-up element the coaching staff could toss in if necessary.

"You hungry?" Hawny asked.

"Starving."

"Are you hungry in your balls or your heart?"

"Both."

"Mickey D's?"

Zeb nodded. Hawny pushed the "La Cucaracha" horn and gassed the truck a little faster. For a moment, a sly, happy feeling came into Zeb's blood. Unless he got injured, unless something catastrophic happened, in less than a week he would experience a state championship game. It seemed almost too big to swallow. A nervous bird had begun to flap behind his rib cage, but he didn't mind it. This was a chance, an opportunity, and Zeb felt himself growing into it. No one had talked much about T.T. either, except to say that he had already departed on an afternoon flight to Dallas. Finished. Gone.

Hawny pulled into McDonald's, but before he turned off the truck, Zeb's phone rang. Zeb plucked it out of his pocket and looked at the number. He didn't recognize it. He was about to reject the call when he realized the number said something about Emporia State. He showed Hawny the screen. Hawny shrugged. Zeb hit the Accept button.

"Hello?" he said, ready to hang up immediately if it was a telemarketer.

"Zeb Holowin?"

"Holloway."

"This is Coach Adams from Emporia State University in Kansas. Your coach gave me permission to call you. Is this a good time to have a chat?"

Zeb slipped out of the truck so Hawny wouldn't hear him. He hung his elbow over the side rail of the truck and held his finger up to Hawny.

"Yes, sir," Zeb said.

"I know, I know, I'm probably catching you around dinnertime and I apologize. Have you been to Kansas, Zeb?"

"No, sir."

"Well, I grew up here and I love it, so I'm prejudiced, but a lot of people fall in love with the wide-open spaces. You might be one of them. Who knows?"

Zeb signaled for Hawny to go inside. He held up his hand to say he would be five minutes.

"What are you calling about, Coach . . ."

"Coach Adams. Like the first man in the Garden of Eden. I'm calling about your football future, Zeb. In a roundabout way, I've heard of you. You came across my desk, so to speak. A good friend of mine played football with your Coach Steve over at Kutztown State. Coach Steve heard we might be recruiting quarterbacks and he gave us your name."

"Really?"

"That's why we're talking. I know you're not a starter, but maybe you would have been if you hadn't played behind T.T. Monroe. Am I right about that?"

"Maybe. It's hard to say, but I think so."

"I like your humility. But Coach Steve says you throw a nice ball. He also said you have a good work ethic, so I figured, we figured—the coaching staff here—it's worth a conversation. Are you planning to play football next year, Zeb?"

"I guess not, honestly."

"Look, I don't want to pretend Emporia is Notre Dame. It's a far cry from that. But we play in a nice conference and we have a competitive team. The system is under a new athletic director, so we're shaking the trees, so to speak, to see what falls out of them."

"I understand."

"What I'd like to do is send you some information on Emporia. Just the usual college materials. You could take a look and get back to me. What do you say? Meanwhile, I'll get a film copy of the state game from Coach Steve or someone at your school. We'll see how you make out. Do you feel as though you have a pretty good arm, Zeb?"

"I have a pretty good arm, yes."

"Well, we run a pro set, so we need a quarterback with a strong arm. That's the buy-in price. That's kind of the minimum."

"Okay."

"That's why Coach Steve probably recommended you. He says you have a good arm."

"Well, I hope I do."

"Good to be in touch, Zeb. And good luck on Saturday. Do you think you'll pull it out?"

"I think so."

Coach Adams laughed on the other end of the line.

"That's what I like to hear."

Zeb almost said, *I feel it in my heart and my balls,* but he caught himself. He smiled up at the early-evening sky. He felt good.

He hung up and went inside to find Hawny. Hawny stood at the counter talking to Gabby Roetzheim, a girl in their class. Zeb said hello. Gabby spoke into a little microphone that pressed against her cheek. She nodded at them both and headed back into the kitchen.

"Who was that on the phone?" Hawny asked.

"Some coach."

"From another school?"

"From a college. Emporia or something out in Kansas."

"Is he loving him some Zeb QB-ness?"

"I don't know what's going on. It's crazy."

"Would you say he was more interested in your heart or your balls?"

"Shut up, Hawny."

Gabby swung back over and took their order. Zeb paid. He didn't know why he paid, but it felt like the universe whispered in his ear that he should. As he counted out the cash, he saw a handwritten sign above the milk-shake machines.

Go Raiders. Mash Merrymeeting.

For the first time, he noticed a hundred cups had been hung from the drop ceiling, each one with a little peppy phrase. *Go Raiders. Merrymeeting Won't Be So Merry.* He reached up and punched one of the cups softly and watched it rock back and forth. The whole town had gone crazy.

Zeb pulled up outside Pappy's Ice Cream, leaned over, and looked through the passenger window to see if Stella had already gone inside. He couldn't tell for sure. He slipped the Civic into first and turned off the engine. The rain had finally let up, but the weather had turned cold and frosty. Pappy's window had a huge sign with a pumpkin drawn on it that read *Pumpkin Ice Cream and Lattes Now Here.* The sign had cornstalks bracketing it. Zeb liked seeing the sign and the pumpkin. He liked almost everything about the fall and Thanksgiving and deer season.

He climbed out of the car and looked through the front window of the shop, trying to see Stella. She had texted and asked him to meet her, but she wasn't inside. He pulled out his phone and read the time. It was 7:10. They were both late, but she was later.

He checked for messages. She hadn't left one. He tucked the phone back in his pocket. He told himself to calm down. He told himself to take it level. Just because she'd asked to see him didn't mean she liked him. It didn't mean she felt interest in that way. Zeb didn't know what to think about T.T. leaving that day and Zeb having a date—was it a date?—to see Stella before anything had settled. But he couldn't resist her. It was silly to pretend that he could, so he bent once more and looked through the shop window. The ice cream counter had a dozen paper turkeys taped to the front of it, obviously some sort of project from the elementary school.

He still stood outside the shop when she arrived. She looked beautiful but a bit hurried. She had pulled her hair up on top of her head and she wore a navy pea coat with a white scarf tucked around her neck.

"Why are you standing outside here?" she asked. "Why didn't you go in?"

"I wasn't sure where you were."

"It's weird to wait outside."

He shrugged. "It wasn't a problem."

"I know it's not a problem. It's just funny. It's cold out here."

She waited while he pushed open the door. When she ducked through, he smelled her perfume.

"Would you like an ice cream?" he asked.

He had rehearsed asking that. It had sounded more natural when he rehearsed it. In the light of the ice cream shop, it sounded forced and throaty, like a kid starting to sing and then stopping before he hit his stride.

"I might have a small cone. Are you going to get something?"

"No, I'm trying to eat right for the game."

"Well, I don't want to eat alone."

Pappy's wasn't crowded. An elderly couple ate two cones at a small table beside the front window. They held the cones nearly sideways and ate them like corn on the cob. A guy in biking shorts and a helmet had just finished ordering a pumpkin latte. Zeb watched the transaction, trying not to give away that he had his hand on the change in his pocket. He had $7.37. He had said he didn't want an ice cream because he wasn't sure what Stella would order or what it might cost, and he wanted to save them both from embarrassment. He calculated he had enough for one ice cream, but probably not two, and he wished that he hadn't sprung for Hawny's hamburger earlier in the evening.

"I guess I don't care. I'm going to have a cone. Strawberry," she said to the girl behind the counter. The counter girl had silver piercings through her nose and brows and top lip. Her short hair shone black, black-black. She looked pretty, Zeb thought. She looked like an exotic bird somehow blown into the wrong habitat. Her clothes were black, too, except for a pair of bright white Converse sneakers that squeaked a little on the linoleum floor as she worked. Maybe away from work, she was kind of a goth, but not really, Zeb judged. Standing across the counter from Stella, the girl looked like coffee while Stella was more like weak tea. Any girl who wore Converse sneakers earned points in his book. Zeb knew her from somewhere, but he couldn't say where. He would have bet money on it, though, and he found his eyes went back and forth between the girl and Stella, and that surprised him. A minute before, he wouldn't have thought he could take his eyes off Stella for anything.

"Oh, I'll have a small cone," he said, finishing the addition in his head from the prices on the board against the back wall. "Vanilla butterscotch, please."

He pulled out a load of the change from his pocket. It nearly slipped out of his hands. He put it on the counter beside the cash register and sorted some of the quarters to one side. He had five dollars in quarters, the rest in dimes and nickels and pennies. He smelled Stella beside him. He smelled her lip gloss and a pepperminty odor he couldn't place.

"So T.T.'s gone," Stella said as he counted. "Completely gone. It's too bizarre."

"Did you guys talk about him leaving?"

"T.T. didn't talk about stuff like that. That wasn't him at all. He's all surface and on to the next thing. He's just that way."

The girl with the piercings handed a strawberry cone to Stella. Stella pulled a napkin out of a dispenser and thanked her. The girl started digging Zeb's ice cream out of the freezer. Her sneakers squeaked. Zeb looked over the counter and saw the girl wore a bright blue fanny pack. It was such an uncool thing to wear that it struck him as pretty interesting.

"I guess I don't get how you guys were together. You and T.T. I thought you were serious."

"We're too young to be serious, Zeb. T.T. knew that. I'll give him that much."

She licked her cone. A small dribble crawled down over her knuckles. She wiped it away with a napkin. At the same time, the counter girl handed him his ice cream. His cone wore a brown cap of butterscotch.

"Are you Zeb Hollo-something?" the girl asked. "Did you go to Franklin Elementary?"

"Yes. Zeb Holloway."

"I'm Ferron Ellis. We were in second grade together."

"With Mrs. Shapiro?"

"Yep. And the art teacher, what was his name? Bazo or something like that."

"Mr. Bazille."

Zeb saw her now. She came into focus. Ferron Ellis had been a heavy girl in second grade. She had been friends with another girl, Bethany Lewis, who was also large. Everyone called them Tank and Truck, but he couldn't remember which was which. Ferron Ellis had lost all that weight. He wondered where the rest of her had gone.

She took his change, sliding the coins into her open palm until she had enough. She talked as she counted.

"I came back about two weeks ago. My father moved into his father's old place in Rumney and I'm living with him now. It sucks to be back. I used to live in Phoenix, which was much nicer. Much."

"Okay," Zeb said, feeling he should introduce Stella but also feeling acutely embarrassed. He knew his face had flushed. He left the coins on the counter as a tip and smiled to show it was for her. "Nice to see you again, Ferron."

"Nice to see you, Zeb."

"She was hitting on you," Stella whispered when they slid into the fountain table at the other side of the door from the couple eating cones. "She's probably had a crush on you for a long, long time."

"I doubt it."

"You're cute, Zeb. You don't know it about yourself and that makes you even cuter."

"Why did you want to meet with me?" he asked, feeling reckless. Sometimes Stella's attention made him feel that way. "I mean, how come?"

She smiled. He liked when she smiled.

"Because I like talking to you. I don't know. We're friends, aren't we? Does there have to be a big reason to meet for an ice cream?"

"Don't you miss T.T.?"

She looked at him curiously.

"He's been gone only a few hours, Zeb."

"Still."

"You have to learn to lighten up, Zeb. I thought it might be nice to get together, that's all. You're acting kind of weird."

"So that's what this is?"

He couldn't get his mind to slow down. They had never gone out at night before. Now that T.T. had left, suddenly she had asked to see him. He couldn't figure it. It seemed like she could trade in T.T. for another guy in the course of one day. He didn't know if it was fair to think that, but that's what it felt like. He might have been a backup on the field, but he wasn't willing to be one in the rest of his life.

"Anyway," she said with a big breath.

"Well, it must have been tough to say goodbye."

"T.T. was complicated, you know? It wasn't always fun being with him. He needed a ton of attention and so do I. I know I do. Don't look at me like that."

Zeb smiled. He was surprised to hear she knew that about herself.

"Life seems dull sometimes," she said. "For me, anyway. One day is pretty much like the next and I hate that. It's all vanilla. As soon as school is over, I'm heading to Hollywood. I am. T.T. leaving made me realize it. I guess that's why I wanted to talk to you."

"I don't know the first thing about Hollywood, Stella."

"I know that, Zeb. I'm not dumb. I want some excitement in

my life, that's all. You get excited going deer hunting, but I need something more. T.T. and I were a lot alike."

"It's good that you know what you want."

"Do you think it's shallow? You probably do."

"No judgment, Stella."

"Oh, you judge. Everyone judges. I hate when people say no judgment."

"I try not to judge."

"What do you think of me?"

She asked it so suddenly that he understood she had wanted to ask it for a while. He looked at her over the ice cream cone. He tried to imagine what sort of answer could satisfy her. He had never seen this side of her. She seemed rattled by T.T.'s departure, maybe slightly nervous about being on her own again.

"You're nice."

"I mean more than that, Zeb. Nice is boring."

"I don't know. I don't know you all that well."

"Do you think I'm pretty?"

He nodded.

"But, like, Hollywood-pretty? Or just like cute enough for Rumney, New Hampshire? Seriously. I don't know if I'm seeing myself accurately."

"This is the weirdest conversation I've ever had."

"I need a guy's opinion!"

"You're pretty, Stella. I don't know how I can quantify that."

"You've watched movies. Do you think I look like the girls in those pictures?"

"I have no idea, Stella."

"I mean, they have makeup people and all that. Hair and clothes. In some ways, it's all different."

"You should ask a girl. I don't know."

"I'm just worried I'm kidding myself. T.T. always said I was New Hampshire–pretty, whatever that is. But he didn't worry about anyone except himself. I never knew how serious he was being."

"You're fine, Stella."

"See? No one wants to tell you the truth. Life is so annoying that way. Why can't we all talk more honestly about things?"

"I don't even know what you're asking, Stella."

"I'm thinking about next year. I'm thinking about going to Hollywood and I need an honest opinion."

"And you're asking me? The most backward sort of guy you know?"

"You're not backward."

"I'm not what you would call hip either. You should be easier on yourself. You should. Things will happen the way they need to happen."

"I don't believe that for a second, Zeb. Not one second. You have to push and grind and make things happen. That's what I've learned. Don't you know that yet?"

"I don't know what I know. I really don't."

Her eyes got teary. Zeb had no clue what had brought that on. He wished he could think of a thing to say that would make her feel better.

"Listen, I have to get going," he said finally, biting the last of his cone and sticking his tongue into the hollow tube. It felt like putting a hat on his tongue. "My mom needs the car back."

Ferron used a white rag on the top of the counter. She put a lot of effort into it, Zeb could tell. He liked people who did work the right way. He had learned that from Uncle Pushee.

Stella stood and walked to the trashcan at the side of the store and tossed her ice cream away. She plucked more napkins out of a wall dispenser and wiped her hands as she crossed back toward him. She slid into the seat across from him. She threw the balled-up napkins at him. She did it playfully, but underneath it Zeb sensed something else. Something had changed between them. Maybe it was anger; he couldn't say for sure.

"Anyhow," she said, "T.T.'s gone and that's that."

"I guess."

"And football season is finished next week. Then we cheer basketball. At least it's warmer."

"That must be better."

She shrugged. He wondered if he had disappointed her. She liked drama and big scenes and he wasn't the guy to give her that. Maybe T.T. supplied her with that. Zeb didn't know the first thing to think. Not the first thing. He stood and waited while she got up. Ferron said goodbye in a voice loud enough for both of them to hear.

"Bye," Zeb said, "nice seeing you again."

"You too," Ferron said.

"She wants your body," Stella said before she went through the door. "Trust me on that. Girls know these things."

"You're full of it."

"You are so naïve, Zeb."

Outside, Zeb walked her to her car. She slid in behind the steering wheel before the question of a kiss or anything else could arise. He felt relieved. What had she wanted, anyway? Why had she asked to see him? He had glimpsed a strange side of her and it made it awkward between them.

"T.T. didn't say goodbye," she said, looking straight ahead at the windshield. "He just messaged me and said he'd see me sometime. We dated for almost a year and he left without even calling to say goodbye."

"That's too bad. Sorry. That probably hurt."

"He was injured, I know. But he left in a really cold way. Poof, he's gone. That's why I was asking all those questions."

"You're pretty, Stella."

She looked at him and smiled. Then she started her car and backed out. He waved. *Raiders Are Rad* was written in blue washable paint across the rear bumper. She held her hand out the window and waved.

Holloway sucks.

He hasn't even played. How would you know, ass-hat?

Without Monroe, you're dead. He was your hol offenze.

Learn to spell, moron.

Merrymeeting will kill you idiots.

Ass-hat.

Trust me.

TUESDAY 4

Zeb sat down in the chair opposite the reporter from the *North Country News,* a local paper that covered the Rumney Raiders. Coach K knew the reporter from way back and had set up a mini–press day in the visitors' locker room before practice. Zeb took his place as the third player interviewed. The sole reason, Zeb knew, he had been asked for an interview was his sudden promotion to starting quarterback.

The reporter didn't look up at first when Zeb sat. He had a skirt of messiness that seemed to come with him; his faux-leather messenger bag sagged open with a yellow pad and a half-eaten sub sandwich from Ginger's.

"Okay, Zeb . . . you're starting this weekend, is that right?" the reporter asked, checking his recording app as he did so. "How's that feel?"

"Feels good. I wish T.T. could play."

"Is it strange to find yourself in this position? At the end of the season?"

"A little, yes, I guess."

"What do you bring to the game?"

Zeb turned red. He moved his feet so that both of his cleats would rest on the concrete floor of the visitors' locker room.

"I just do my best."

"But how do you see yourself in the context of the game?"

Zeb felt his tongue had turned into a frog, and the frog had its head facing the wrong way, down toward Zeb's heart.

"I don't know. Really, I try to keep the offense moving. Coach K calls the plays, so I just run them."

"But you might switch a play at the line? Audible? Isn't that possible?"

"It's rare. But I can do that. This is all a little new. But if I see an opening, yes, sure, I can change the play."

The man pulled the yellow pad from his bag. Zeb shifted on the chair. The reporter smiled at him.

"Do you know what Truman said after FDR died? He said he felt like a ton of hay had fallen on his head. That's how you must be feeling taking over for T.T."

"That's about right."

"Is that your dad who runs the body shop out on Redtree Road?"

"My uncle."

"George Pushee?"

"Yes."

"I know George. If I can ask, how come your last name is Holloway?"

"I have my mom's name. After my dad left, we kind of went back to that. That won't be in the paper, though, will it?"

"No, just my own curiosity. Small-town living."

"Yes, sir."

"Okay, Zeb, good luck on Saturday. Will you send the next fellow in?"

Zeb stood. He started to move, then he stopped.

"I'm going to do okay," he said to the man.

The man looked at him and smiled.

"I bet you will," he said.

Zeb watched Jimbo roll left, fake a pass to his wide-out, then tuck the ball under his right arm and start to run. The defense wore yellow vests and the D-players—scrubs and nut-squadders like Hawny—came forward and only put their hands up to touch Jimbo as he went around the left end. Jimbo pretended to straight-arm the defense away. Playing defensive safety, Hawny came forward and popped his fist on Jimbo's shoulder pads. The blow made a funny thwacking sound and Hawny danced away, laughing.

"Run it again," Coach Hoch shouted. "Run it back and run it again."

The players regrouped. Jimbo trotted back and tossed the ball to Coach Steve. Coach Steve placed the ball on the thirty-yard line. Coach Larentino put his foot on it and blew a whistle to start the play clock. Coach K stood off to one side. The reporter, Joe Eastman—Zeb now recalled his name—stood beside the coach. They talked out of the sides of their mouths and kept their eyes on the practice. If horses could talk while they looked over a fence, Zeb thought, they would talk as Coach K and Joe Eastman talked.

Zeb pushed his hands down the front of his pants. He felt cold. The practice had gone on too long. The weather report called for snow on Thursday, Thanksgiving Day. Uncle Pushee would like that, Zeb reflected. First snow could be a deer snow, a way to make tracking easier. As Uncle Pushee always said, a deer couldn't fly, so if you had legs to follow him, you could usually see where he went. George Pushee. That's what Joe Eastman had called him. George Pushee of Redtree Road. Redtree Road said a lot about anyone who lived there, Zeb knew. Redtree Road wasn't the best part of town. In the old days, they called it the Dump Road, but then some people demanded it be changed so that land values wouldn't be influenced by such a cruddy name. It was still the Dump Road to most people, though. Zeb understood that. Redtree Road was like a blue tarp you put over something to try to keep the weather out.

Zeb turned his attention back to Jimbo calling cadence. Jimbo had a surprisingly high voice for a big guy. When the ball came into his hands, he faked to the halfback, Otzman, then swung left, looking downfield. The defense fanned out, guarding receivers. When Jimbo tucked the ball under his arm, the defense swarmed forward. They looked like seagrass to Zeb, motion taking them back and forth.

Jimbo ran like a big, frightened moose. His legs ticked out a little down by the knees, so he looked splayed and slightly clumsy. Still, he covered ground, and by the time he had made it around the left end, he had a head of steam going. When Hawny came forward, Jimbo smacked him as hard as he could in the face with a poleax straight-arm, payback for Hawny smacking his shoulder pads on the previous play. Hawny had been going only half speed, so Jimbo's extra force knocked Hawny's head back and crumpled him. A hoot of pleasure went up from the other players—it always did after a good, vicious hit—and Jimbo turned around to face Hawny, then skipped backwards and taunted him. For his part, Hawny lay on the ground and hardly moved. He looked like a pile of laundry someone had left out in a rain.

Before he knew what he intended to do, Zeb sprinted at Jimbo and launched himself at the bigger boy. Zeb didn't care what happened or what price he had to pay for such an action. His friend had just been injured, and taunted on top of that, and the unfairness of the exchange—one kid going half speed, the other full—made something burn in Zeb's chest and throat. He knew, even as he stuck his helmet in the center of Jimbo's numbers and tackled him to the ground, that it had something to do with Redtree Road, with being dismissible, with knocking Hawny around because Hawny was an insignificant nut-squadder who had practiced every day for three years but never played a single down.

"Get off me!" Jimbo shouted and nearly bucked Zeb off. Jimbo was strong as anything, strong as a python. Zeb had no chance of keeping him down.

"Say you're sorry," Zeb shouted into Jimbo's face.

But that was the end of it. Suddenly Zeb felt himself pulled away. Coach Steve and some of the other players separated them. Zeb didn't resist. He didn't want to fight Jimbo. He didn't even feel angry, particularly. You just couldn't do what Jimbo had done to a friend of his and get away with it.

"Take a lap, Holloway," Coach Hoch suddenly shouted into his face. "Take ten. Run until I tell you to stop, damn it."

Jimbo chucked the ball at Zeb. Zeb felt it bounce off his

shoulder pads. He didn't care. He stopped quickly to check on Hawny. Hawny grinned. He was okay. Zeb gave him his hand and pulled him up.

"Just quit," Zeb whispered to Hawny. "Don't put up with this."

Hawny grabbed his arm and pulled him away. Zeb broke into a slow trot beside his friend.

"You went Beast Mode on that guy," Hawny said. "On old Jimbo. My man!"

"If you weren't such a sissy I wouldn't have had to."

"Did you feel angry in your heart or your balls?"

Zeb couldn't help laughing. He jogged next to Hawny. He didn't care if he had to face repercussions for fighting with a teammate. Coach K could bench him and it didn't matter because you had to do certain things when certain things happened. That's all it was.

Coach Steve jogged up to them before they made it back to the squad. Practice had ended anyway. The players trotted off toward the locker room. Zeb looked for the reporter and saw him walking toward the street beyond the field house. He carried a big black bag over one shoulder, the messenger bag over the other.

"What a pair of dopes," Coach Steve said, grinning. "What's wrong with you two?"

"We're woodchucks," Hawny said. "New Hampshire hillbillies."

"Yeah, I'll say you're woodchucks. Get out of here, Hawny. Let me talk to Zeb for a minute."

Hawny made a funny face and jogged away. Zeb stopped next to Coach Steve. Coach Steve had enough warmth going that his body smoked a little in the cold evening air. He wore his Kutztown State sweatshirt and a baseball hat that said CERISSAMO LUMBER YARD in red lettering across the cap's front. Coach Steve looked young and strong and fit. He could do two hundred pushups, Zeb knew. Everyone on the team knew that.

"You can't be fighting, Zeb," Coach Steve said, turning to walk next to him. "You're the QB. QBs don't fight. They bring the team together. You can't be fighting this week especially."

"I know. Sorry."

"Patch it up with Jimbo when you go inside, will you? Don't let this hang around and grow sour. It could spoil things for this week."

"Yes, sir."

"Hawny's your boy, huh?"

"Yes, sir. I guess so."

"I don't blame you. Personally, I hate these half-speed drills. No one's ever sure how fast to go and something like this always ends up happening."

Zeb nodded. That was true. They came to the edge of the running track and stopped. Someone had put fresh pine pallets down across the running surface early in the year and the pallets had become dented and splintered from all the cleats going across it day after day.

"While I have you," Coach Steve said, "did you get a call from Emporia State?"

"Yes, sir. I meant to thank you for that."

"Well, you're welcome. Coach Adams, right?"

Zeb nodded.

"I don't know much about the program, honestly. A friend is involved with it, but that's the way things happen sometimes. Somebody lets you in and you grab an opportunity."

"Yes, sir."

"You know, I had a background a lot like yours, Zeb. Came up the same way. My mom ran a dry-cleaning shop. Managed it. That's where I worked every summer. Football really helped me. It paved the way for some things."

Zeb nodded.

"Just stay levelheaded for the next week. No big decisions, okay? Get enough rest and get to school on time. You're doing a good job in practice. Are you resentful about Jimbo playing some reps at QB?"

"Not really."

"That's what it looked like when you went after him like you did. That's why you have to make it cool between you."

"Yes, sir."

"This could be a big week in your life, you know? You know that, don't you?"

Zeb looked away and then back at Coach Steve. He nodded.

"Are you thinking about college, Zeb? What's your plan for next year?"

"No one in my family has ever gone to college."

"I don't believe college is for everyone, but it might be a good steppingstone for you. A school like Emporia . . . I don't know. It's small and you'd have a place there. You could do worse and it could get you off to a good start."

"Yes, sir."

"Do you want to stay local and have that kind of life?"

"I don't think so. I never thought too much about it. I never knew there might be a way out. I like this town, this area. But I don't think I want to spend the rest of my life working in my uncle's shop."

"You probably should start thinking about it, Zeb. The future, I mean. If you don't have a plan, the world will plan for you, believe me. It's up to you to pick a direction. You should go in and see some of the guidance counselors. They may help you figure out some of your options."

"I never thought I had many options."

"Don't get in your own way. Don't say no to yourself. Don't be an obstacle to yourself—that makes no sense. School will be over before you know it, believe me. Then you have to fall back on your plan. If you don't have a plan . . . you see the problem?"

"Yes, sir."

"Even if college isn't great, it forces you to look at how you want to live. You see new things, meet new people. It changes your perspective. Maybe that's the whole point of college. It broadens you."

Zeb nodded.

"The world isn't just Grafton County, New Hampshire, Zeb. The world is wide. I have a feeling you could do pretty well out in that world, but you have to get there first. You have to knock on the door. Even if it's not Emporia, you could go somewhere. Not to play football, necessarily, but to change your history, if you know what I mean."

"I know what you mean."

"And none of this is a criticism of how you live now. If that's what you want, if that makes you happy, then stay with it. But be sure you are making a choice about it. An informed choice. Then decide, okay?"

"Yes, sir."

"You're a good kid, Zeb. I know you. I know what it's like in your heart. I was just like you."

Zeb looked away and then back at the coach. No one had ever said a thing like that to him. Coach Steve slapped him on the shoulder pads and that was that. Zeb jogged off, first stepping across the wooden pallet as you might step across boulders crossing a stream.

"Look at all this swag," Hawny said, digging into the bag of treats Zeb's "little sister" had provided. "This is balls, man. You got some girl you don't even know giving you candy?"

"I guess so."

"That's so weird."

"What does she get out of it?"

"No idea."

"Chicks are strange. They actually like this kind of stuff. You imagine a guy creeping around with a bag of candy, trying to put it secretly into a girl's locker?"

"I can't even picture them buying the candy. And writing a little note? No way."

"I love girls. I love that they do this shit. It's so freaking crazy."

Hawny opened a Kit Kat bar and ate it in about two bites. Then his hand went back into the bag. He had the truck at a stop sign in the center of town. It was the long way home. Hawny sometimes liked to go through town instead of taking the back roads.

"And look at this crap!" Hawny said, bending to look up at the wire suspended over the road. "They've got banners everywhere! This town has a complete boner for this game."

"I know. I don't get it."

"You better get it. You're the QB, ace. You like fireballs? Fireballs are like dwarf balls. Dwarf balls with jock itch."

Zeb laughed. He dug in the bag and pulled out a mini–chocolate bar. He felt good. He felt tired but good. It occurred to him that at this time four days from now, the game would be over. Win, lose, or draw, it would be over. In four days, he would be looking back at the game. Whatever happened, it would be behind him.

The light changed and Hawny drove ahead.

"What are you going to do when you graduate?" Zeb asked. "You have any idea?"

"I told you. I'm going to be a Marine."

"Are you serious, though?"

"Hell yeah," Hawny said, digging in for more candy. "Why not? I'm going to hump my twenty years and then retire. You should do it with me."

"I don't know."

"We would be sooooo badass."

"I never really thought much about the future. I never thought much about the next thing."

"You should go to college. Get the freak out of here."

"You don't like Rumney?"

"I like Rumney, but there's nothing for us to do here. Not really. It's dead around here. That's why everyone has a boner for the game."

"You might be right."

"I am right! You think people with other things to do get such a boner for a high school football game?"

"People like football."

"Sure they do. But having a good team lets them think they're doing something right. The townspeople, I mean. If we have a good football team, then we must have a good school system. Shit like that."

"You're cold, Hawny."

"Calling it like it is."

Hawny looked over and snagged a sleeve of Smarties. He stuck the whole package in his mouth, chewed it for a second, then reached in and pulled out the plastic wrapping. He chucked the wrapping out of the window. He looked over and smiled. He opened his mouth to show all the Smarties. His tongue was blue.

"Nobody is ever going to care how we did in class, what we learned, what time we wasted going to this school, but they will remember the football game. They'll put a team picture and a trophy in the trophy case. You'll be looking out at some kid fifty years from now. Everyone can say, 'See? They won the state championship. Look at these noble young men!'"

"What's your point, Hawny?"

"My point is you need to get the hell out of Dodge next spring. Don't be the asshole booster standing in the bleachers watching the high school team practice twenty years from now. You got to get out of here."

"You will be the world's most badass Marine."

"You telling me? Who's the best shot in, like, the top half of the state?"

"You are."

"That's right. Give me some more dwarf balls. She just put this candy in there for kicks?"

T.T. Monroe ain't signed with USC now, jerkhead.

He'll fix his knee.

You don't fix something like that. Game over.

People come back.

Whatever chance he had is over. Yesterday's news.

He's still better than Holloway. Even on one leg.

Hell yeah.

"So you're playing quarterback, huh?" Ferron asked.

He nodded. He watched Ferron scoop his ice cream out of one of the vats.

"And this is the big game . . . this Saturday?" she asked, straightening. She held the cone out to him. He had asked for a small cone, but she had put a second scoop on top.

"I just wanted a small cone, Ferron."

"I know. But it's on the house. I'll have to charge you for the cone, though. The first scoop."

"Sure."

"But the second scoop is on me. Or on the shop, I should say."

She smiled. He smiled back. He wasn't entirely sure how he had ended up in Pappy's talking to Ferron. He had things to do at home, some homework too, but he had borrowed his mom's car and driven down for an ice cream as if it couldn't be postponed another day. He hadn't been exactly thinking of Ferron, but she had somehow come up in his mind in a way he used to reserve for

Stella. He hadn't even known if Ferron would be working. He had nothing planned and no script to follow. Ferron. Tank, he remembered. They used to call her Tank.

"So what's your story?" Ferron asked as she poured his change into his palm. "Are you with that girl from the other night?"

"What girl?" he asked, then immediately told himself he was a dumb ass to pretend he didn't understand what she meant.

"That girl. The pretty girl you were with."

"No, she's the old quarterback's girlfriend. Was. It's complicated."

"One of those, eh?" Ferron asked. "One of those complex affairs."

"It's hardly an affair."

"Look at you blush! I thought you were such a tough guy when you were little. You were like a wild animal. I used to think you lived in the woods, maybe in a tree hollow or something."

"You mean that?" Zeb asked, taking a lick of his ice cream. Chocolate marshmallow. He looked around. The place was empty. It was dinnertime, really, so that explained it. Ice cream was going to be his dinner, he decided.

"Yeah, you seemed older than the other boys. Like you took care of yourself already," she said. "You know, of all the boys, you were the only one who didn't call me by that name. Call me fat. That always stuck with me. You didn't pile on and tease me. That teasing really hurt."

"I'm sorry."

"Sometimes they circled us like dogs—the boys, I mean—and I would look around and the only one who wasn't joining in was you. I'll always remember that."

"Boys can be mean."

"They can be cruel. They can be really cruel. You weren't, though."

Zeb didn't know what to say to that. She changed the subject.

"So this is the state championship game? Do you play teams from other states?"

"No, it's to be the New Hampshire state champion."

"Okay, cool. You like football, then, huh?"

"It's pretty fun."

"I'd be afraid I'd get hurt. All that running into each other. You know that can't be good for your brain, right?"

"I know."

"Funny that schools promote a sport that can kill your brain. They spend all day trying to stuff your brain with knowledge, then they tell you to go out and smack your head into someone else and risk losing it all. I'd call that a contradiction."

"People don't think about it that way."

"Well, I do. I'm a person."

"I mean the general—"

"The general public? Who is the general public? That's what I want to know."

She smiled. Her smile broke quick and fast across her face like a flashlight splashing its beam into a mirror.

"I'll be sure to tell Coach K," he answered weakly. "Maybe the game will be called off on account of Ferron Ellis."

"My dad says I am too quick to get on my soapbox, but that's the way I am. I pick at things."

"That's a good trait," Zeb said.

"Do you think so?"

"Sure. So, will you come to the game?"

"I doubt it. No reflection on you, but it's not my thing."

"I understand."

"I thought you were with that girl the other night. I told my dad when I went home that I had run into you and that you were with a date."

"It wasn't a date, that's for sure."

"What are you doing for Thanksgiving?" she asked, wiping down the counters between the ice cream vats. "The reason I ask is my dad is big on Thanksgiving. He has a bunch of food that he always cooks and it's his mission to make sure everyone in the world has a seat at his table. He says that's the true meaning of Thanksgiving."

"I don't know what I'm doing yet," Zeb fibbed. "Depends on family."

"Sure, no, I get it. Just, if you want to come over, we eat at four sharp. That's the rule. You might like it. My dad's a pretty good guy and he's way into sports. He'd probably like to talk to you. And the food is always great."

"Would it be a date?" Zeb asked, then immediately regretted cracking such a stupid joke.

"I wasn't thinking it was a date, Zeb. Just a meal."

"Sorry."

"Swing by if you like. Here, I'll write down my number and address. Even if you just come for a slice of pie, it will be okay. We have a full house, usually."

She wrote something on an old receipt and handed it to him. He didn't recognize the street. He folded it and put it in his wallet.

He never knew how a conversation needed to end. He raised the ice cream cone in thanks.

"See you," he said.

"Bye, Zeb."

"I'm glad you're back in town, Ferron."

"You didn't even know I was gone."

"But now I know you're back."

She smiled.

"I *was* thinking it was a date, sort of," she said.

"Really?"

She shrugged. He walked out and finished the ice cream so fast it gave him a headache. When he got back in the car, he sat for a minute and looked up and down the main street of town. The biggest banner hung dead in the middle of the main intersection. It said GO RUMNEY! On one side, someone had drawn a picture of a Raider. The other side gave the time and date of the game and said it would be broadcast on WBZA out of Concord. Coverage started at nine o'clock Saturday morning.

Zeb slowly reached forward and started the car. It choked a little before settling into its rhythm. He backed up and drove carefully through town. He rolled down the window and let the cold air find him. Zeb envied Stella and Hawny. They knew exactly what they wanted to do next. Maybe he needed to go to college. People talked about college as if everyone knew what it was, but he didn't. He didn't have a clue, really. He knew you went to classes and he knew you studied, but that was about all. It was just a word: *college.* It was like saying *apple* or *peach* or *town.* And if he didn't go to college, what then? He could work with Uncle Pushee, but he couldn't imagine doing that full-time.

He drove to the Rumney football stadium and parked outside it. Ironically, no one had bothered to decorate the place where they practiced. He climbed out of the car and walked through the concession area, then onto the field. An old guy jogged around the running track, his dog following him. Zeb liked the feeling of the grass under his feet. He walked to the fifty-yard line. A football field wasn't very big, when you got right down to it. Not to a deer hunter. It was the size of a small meadow he knew up by Three Ponds. He didn't pretend to run a play or do anything at all like that. He merely stood and looked around. The moon had already risen.

"Zeb, honey? Is that you?"

Zeb stepped through the squeaky door of the camper. He hung up his jacket and kicked off his shoes. At least the camper felt cozy. His mom must have had the wood stove going for a while to make it so warm, Zeb reflected. She also had candles lit. He smelled the candles right away. She liked lighting candles when Arthur stopped by.

"Look at what came for you today!" she said from the couch.

The couch was also his bed. Arthur sat on the other side of the couch, a little farther from the wood stove. They both held drinks of pale peach-colored liquid and milky ice cubes. Zeb crossed over and took the package that his mom held out to him. It was a large envelope with an Emporia State sticker on the back. It was easily the biggest piece of mail, the thickest, that he had ever received.

"Looks like a college has an interest in you," Arthur said, his voice square and careful, the way it could get after a couple of drinks. "Emporia. Where is that? Is that Upstate New York?"

"Kansas," Zeb said, still judging the weight of the package. It was a bubble envelope. A small gash gaped at the bottom where something had punctured it. Zeb put it on the counter next to the sink and went to the refrigerator and opened the door. He wasn't hungry, exactly, but he didn't want to keep talking to his mother and Arthur about the package. He wanted to open it when he was alone. If he opened it now, he knew, the package would lose something and he wouldn't be able to get it back.

"Open it, Zebby!" his mom said. "They thought enough of you to overnight it. How about that? They must be serious! When it came, I tried to remember if I had ever received an overnight package . . . I'm not sure I have, honestly. I can't call one to mind. I don't think any of my business has ever been urgent enough or that anyone I knew had enough money to spend it on an overnight mailing . . ."

She used her cheerful voice. It was the voice he imagined her using at the Fish Bowl after her second margarita. Arthur stood. He could read a situation better than his mother; Zeb had to hand him that. Besides, it was obvious they were both sitting in the place where he had to go to bed eventually. Arthur was good about understanding the constrictions in the camper. Arthur knew what couldn't be changed.

"Let him open it in his own time," Arthur said, matching his tone to Zeb's mom's voice. "I'm going to clear out of here. I just meant to stop by for a quick one. Ziggy Marley needs a walk at home. Little dogs are easy in some ways, but they sure have tiny bladders."

"You sure you don't want another, Art?"

"Positive. Thank you. Don't want to take on too much ballast before sailing, if you know what I mean. Zeb, how's the team looking?"

Zeb pulled out of the refrigerator holding a small Greek yogurt. He didn't really want it, but he needed something in his hands.

"We're looking pretty good," Zeb said. "We should be ready."

"I like hearing that," Arthur said. "That's great."

"You're being a party pooper, Zebby. Aren't you curious what they sent?"

"I'll look at it eventually."

"I'd like to see it," his mom said. "Don't I count for anything?"

The same voice she had employed before, Zeb noted. It was her Arthur voice, girlish and slightly needy. But she didn't push it. She stood and followed Arthur out. Zeb opened the yogurt and ate it in the rocking chair next to the stove. He heard Arthur's car start, then his mom reappeared. She sat on the couch and tucked her legs under her. Zeb felt sleepy from the warmth. He didn't like denying his mom the pleasure of seeing the package opened, but he also felt he couldn't give in. He felt like he might lose something important if he opened it too quickly. Whatever was good inside it might flitter away.

"Zeb, honey, I need to tell you that I am doing everything I can to get free on Saturday, but it's not going to be easy."

"It's okay, Mom."

"Not really, it's not. It's the damn holiday. Sorry. I have racked my head to try to think of a way of getting free. People who put in for Thanksgiving off are traveling. We cover for each other and I put in to cover a long time back, and now that I need a day . . . well, we don't have many girls to cover for us. For me."

"Honestly, Mom, it's okay. You didn't know this was going to happen."

"No, that's true, I didn't. But the truth is my son isn't going to start in a state championship game too many times in his life. I'm so proud of you, Zeb. So deeply proud."

Her eyes filled. Zeb put the empty yogurt container on the table in front of the couch and scooted over to sit next to his mom. She started crying harder and she put her face in her hands. He smelled liquor on her, but that wasn't it. He knew it went deeper. It went into the walls of the ridiculous camper that bowed and rocked and made metal buckling sounds whenever the wind pushed hard enough. It went into the absurd dimensions of the camper, the fact they had to remain plugged into Uncle Pushee's house with a long orange extension cord. It went into the exhaustion that lived in her hands and back and in her eyes, and the humiliation she felt each time she had to borrow some money from Arthur or delay paying a bill. He felt himself getting close to tears merely sitting beside her.

"Mom, it's okay. It really is. I'd love for you to be there, but if you can't, I understand."

She fell onto his chest and shook her head hard. Her tears seeped through her body. After a while she sat up. He slid away and grabbed a paper towel and handed it to her. She wiped her eyes and snuffled.

"Maybe if I can't . . . maybe we could get the video of it and you would sit beside me and we could watch it together . . . maybe you could tell me everything, Zebby, everything you thought or felt and it would almost be like I was there. I bet Coach K would do that. If I can't come, would you do that with me? Do you promise me?"

"Of course, Mom."

"I meant to be a better mom, Zeb. I really did. Things just ganged up on me and I lost my way. You know, I never intended to stay here in this camper. It was just supposed to be a temporary fix. And here I am all these years later."

She fell back against him, crying harder still. He let her stay there. He thought about his father, Lawrence, vaulting over the fence. He wondered if his father understood what it meant to go away from the family you had just started, how betrayed trust wasn't a wound likely to heal in a trailer beside a body shop on Redtree Road.

Later, after his mother went to bed, Zeb grabbed the package off the counter and carried it to his bed on the couch. He turned the envelope around so that the address stood out properly: vertical and well sized. It pleased him to look at his address on the paper label in the center of the packet. It pleased him, too, to see the overnight tape that UPS had wrapped around the entire mailing. He couldn't help recalling all the packages that had arrived at Coach K's office for T.T. on an almost a daily basis. Compared to that level of interest, his own package appeared meager. Nevertheless, the package came from a college, came from a coach, and seeing it rest on his lap put a small fire in his heart.

Zeb opened the top of the envelope and shook out the contents slowly. Brochures, mostly. He picked them up, one by one, and examined them briefly. They contained a sameness that surprised him. In almost every brochure someone had taken pictures of young people doing various activities: studying, looking at microscopes, running on a track. Different departments around the college sponsored each brochure. The athletic brochure had a glossy cover that displayed a picture of a female volleyball player spiking over the net.

Zeb put everything back in the envelope. He found a note from Coach Adams as he put the last brochures inside. The note, written on Emporia State letterhead, said, *Good luck on Saturday, Zeb. We'll be in touch.* That was all. Coach Adams had signed his first name: Ted.

WEDNESDAY 5

"Stella, wait, wait, sorry, wait," he said.

She looked up at him. They had just kissed. It was nothing like Zeb imagined it would be. It felt like they were both pretending. It felt like Barbie and Ken mashing their lips together.

"Really?" she asked.

"I don't know. This doesn't feel . . ."

"You're saying it doesn't feel good?"

"No, it feels amazing."

"Then . . ." She reached for him, but not with any conviction.

Zeb ringed her wrist with his fingers and slowly drew her hand away. Stella looked at him.

"You're being serious right now?"

"Sorry."

"Wow."

"It feels funny, that's all."

"I thought you said it felt amazing."

"It does feel amazing, but it feels weird too."

"For God's sake," she said and began pulling herself together. He heard her bracelets jingling. He made room for her in the small AV closet. It was a place she knew about. That was part of the problem. It was someplace she came with T.T. She had a key for the cheerleading office that matched the lock of the AV closet. No one used the AV closet anymore. Its shelves were lined with old projectors and VCR players. It had no windows. The only light came from the slit under the door. Zeb doubted anyone had been inside it in years other than T.T. and Stella.

"Sorry," he said.

He knew he was being a complete idiot. Any guy in the school would have traded places with him in two seconds flat. He didn't know why he was doing it, really, except that he had to.

"Well, this is a first," she said. "Never had a guy complain before."

"I'm not complaining. It's just . . ."

"Are you some religious nut or something?"

"No, not at all."

"What, then?"

He could hardly see her in the dimness of the AV closet. He wondered what in the world he'd intended by stopping her. It *had* felt amazing. It had felt incredible. Then something had changed way back in his mind and he couldn't say what it was except that he had to stop. Hawny would have told him he was a nut, Zeb knew. Anyone would.

"It just felt funny."

"Funny ha-ha? Or funny weird?"

"It didn't feel like it meant anything to you."

"Oh, ass. So now it's my fault."

"It's not your fault. It's nobody's fault. I don't know why I asked you to stop, honestly. Sorry. It's not personal."

"Not personal? What do you mean? What's it supposed to mean, Zeb?"

"Just something."

"This whole thing is reversed. You're the guy and you're telling me to stop."

"I guess."

She took out ChapStick and ran it back and forth over her lips. He could hardly see her. That was part of the problem too. It didn't feel right; it felt like she could have been anyone. Now that she had asked, though, he couldn't think in a straight line.

"Fuck you, Zeb. You know that? Fuck you."

"I'm sorry, Stella. I am."

"You don't know what you're turning down, you idiot. You'll never be the man T.T. is . . . not in here or on the field. You're so stupid it's sickening."

She left in a quick blast. He stood in the darkness feeling like the lowest man on earth. He squared his Carhartt away and stood for a couple breaths collecting himself. He felt confused and ignorant when he stepped outside of the AV closet. Nothing went as you anticipated. That was what he was learning.

The basement hallway was empty. He stood listening to the sound of the building above him. He heard feet pounding the floors and lockers slamming. It was between third and fourth period. He had to hurry. He had left his books in study hall and now the classes had changed and he would be late to biology. He sprinted down the length of the hallway and took the stairs two at a time.

He passed by Otzman on the way to biology. Otzman looked incredibly tough, with a sharp, full chin and deep-set eyes. He looked like pictures of Marines that sometimes appeared on posters around school. He looked like Tarzan or Batman or some combination of both.

Otzman held out his fist for a knuckle-bump as they passed each other.

"State," Otzman said and nodded, his hand hard as a doorknob.

"State," Zeb replied.

Otzman surprised him by stopping him.

"Hey, how are you feeling about all this?" Otzman asked. "You down with everything?"

"It's okay."

"You're doing okay. The guys have talked about it. You're playing fine."

"I'm doing my best."

"We have you covered, man. Next man up, right?"

"Right."

"It's building inside me. I feel like I'm going to pop sometimes."

"We got to keep it steady, though, right?"

Otzman nodded. The guy could storm a machine-gun nest and not get injured, Zeb thought. He looked like a superhero. They didn't run in the same circles except when it came to football, but Zeb had always found him to be a decent guy. He was a champion wrestler. He was going to college on a wrestling scholarship someplace in Pennsylvania. T.T. might have been the star of the team, but Otzman was the stud.

"All right, Zeb, see you at practice."

"Okay."

"Just keep doing what you're doing. Coach K knows how to win."

"I know."

"Later."

Zeb hustled to get to class. The bell rang as he slid into his seat at the lab bench. Fifth period. Three more to go.

Zeb felt his right knee bend out and then back in a short, powerful creak that he knew at once had an echo that he would hear for days and weeks to come. It had been the most innocent of plays, a straight-dive play to Dunham, the fullback, a play designed to get two or three yards in a pinch. It ran over Harper, the right tackle, who was the biggest player on the team, a baby rhino who was fat and sloppy but still had bulk on his side. Zeb didn't know if he'd stepped too far or if Dunham had veered to his left a little, but their knees collided and Dunham kept going, smack into Harper's broad back, then he pivoted sideways and continued on.

All the way around, the timing had been awkward.

Zeb danced away, limping, trying to keep his weight off his right leg. His mind went over his body, racing to his knee to investigate the damage. It couldn't be bad, he told himself. That couldn't happen. Not this week. Not with all he had riding on the game.

"Run it again, run it again," Coach Larentino shouted. "For God's sake, Harper, get your fat ass moving! Get it moving! We're playing for the state championship here!"

Zeb limped to the huddle. Coach Hoch yelled to him. "Zeb, let Jimbo run it. Take a break. Is your leg okay? You okay?"

Zeb limped in a half-circle away from the huddle, then stepped back inside it.

"I'm okay," he said to Coach Hoch.

"Take a break, I said. Just stretch it out."

Zeb's eyes met Dunham's. Dunham's helmet fit strangely. It created a short ridge of flesh at the bottom of his brow. He looked like a wild pig in his helmet.

"Sorry, dude," Dunham said.

"It's okay."

Zeb limped back and let Jimbo take his place. He felt a crazy rush of heat swarm up his body to his scalp. His knee hurt. It hurt a lot. He didn't think he could put weight on it. The trainer, Mrs. Gilmore, came over from the sideline. Zeb had seen this kind of thing happen a hundred times before, but he had never been part of it. Mrs. Gilmore had a short, snappy stride. She taught math and geology during the school day, but she headed up the trainers in the afternoons and Saturdays. Dino walked beside her, carrying the medical box.

"Come over here, Zeb," Mrs. Gilmore said. "Can you put weight on it? Let's move off a little bit."

"I'm okay."

"Doesn't look like you're okay. Come here."

She put her arm around his waist and led him back behind the coaches. To Zeb's surprise, Coach K walked slowly over and stood next to Dino. Coach K didn't say anything.

"What happened?" Mrs. Gilmore asked. "Knee or ankle?"

"Knee."

"Right or left?"

"Right."

"Hit or twisted?"

"Dunham ran into it. Our knees hit and mine went sideways a little."

"Lateral."

"I guess."

Zeb realized a second later that she had been speaking to Dino, teaching him how to make an initial diagnosis.

"Let's get some ice on it. Coach K, I'm going to get him in."

"Okay," Coach K said. "How's it feel, Zeb?"

"It feels fine, honestly."

"We're almost done here today. Tomorrow's a day off, so keep it elevated. We'll see how things look on Friday."

"Yes, sir."

"Let's get an ice pack on it," Mrs. Gilmore said to Dino. "Let's wrap it."

Zeb felt funny walking with Mrs. Gilmore's arm around his waist, but he had to admit he had trouble putting weight on that leg.

Up in the trainers' room, he sat on the end of the taping bench and let Mrs. Gilmore push his pant leg up. It wouldn't go far enough and he had to slide off the bench and slip out of his pants. It felt strange doing that in front of Mrs. Gilmore, but she didn't seem to notice or care. He kept his right leg flexed and up like a dog favoring a paw.

"It's swelling up," Mrs. Gilmore said, taking a closer look at it.

She slid a stool next to the taping table and examined his knee.

"It's just a thing. I'm fine," Zeb said.

"Well, we can't afford to lose you too," she said. "Let's get some ice on it and see where we are. I might send you over to the hospital for x-rays."

"I'll be okay."

"I can't begin to know what's happened inside. I doubt anything is broken, but you hit it hard. Look how swollen it's already become."

Zeb looked at the knee. It hurt and it looked bad.

"Probably sprained. That's what we call things when we don't know for sure what's going on. A sprained knee. Have you been over to the hospital before?"

"No, ma'am."

"I guess you probably need an MRI."

Zeb bent forward and whispered. "My family doesn't have that kind of money, Mrs. Gilmore."

She looked up and smiled. It was a funny kind of smile, Zeb noticed. It wasn't a happy smile. It was a smile of understanding.

"You're a minor. You're covered, Zeb. Healthy Kids. That's the name of the program. It's statewide."

He nodded. Dino arrived with ice and a bunch of bandages.

"Let's ice it for the night and see where we get. Keep it elevated. I think it's just sprained, as I said. I don't think there's anything structurally injured . . ."

Zeb nodded. She prodded the knee a little and checked the kneecap. It turned wherever she touched it.

"You have to stay off it. Dino, let's get this ice on here fast. Is there someone at home to take care of you?"

"Yes, ma'am."

"I'll call you in the morning to check. If you can't move your knee, we'll run you to the doctor's, okay?"

Zeb nodded. He felt ice against his leg. It tickled. He looked at

Dino. Dino held the bandages out like a waiter serving something good to eat. Zeb leaned back on his elbows. If blood had a sound, he heard it in his knee.

Later, close to midnight, his leg throbbed in pulses that matched his blood going through his body. It hurt a lot. He couldn't find a decent position for it. He thought about getting up and trying to stretch it, but he didn't want to wake his mom. He also had Mr. Television on his stomach, the cat's face inches from his own. Mr. Television's breath smelled like onion grass. He rubbed Mr. Television's neck and shoulders. Mr. Television smiled and purred but didn't move.

He reached over the coffee table and grabbed his phone. He texted Stella. He did it fast so he couldn't think about it. *Sorry,* he texted. *Just in a weird place.*

He put the phone back down and rolled onto his side, bracing himself with Mr. Television as he did so. His knee sent out a rattling vibration that felt like a bone under his kneecap banged with a little hammer. A heavy fullness replaced it, a thick, unwieldy pus-filled muscle swell that made him whimper a little as his knee settled. It hurt.

His phone dinged to say a text had come in. He picked it up and read the message. At first it didn't make any sense. It said, *See you tomorrow, I hope. Swing by.*

He read it a second time before he realized it was from Ferron, not Stella. He held the phone away from him to confirm the name. Ferron Ellis had texted him. He didn't even know she had his number.

He typed a message but it came out forced. Stupid humor. He deleted it. Then he concentrated and attempted a different message.

Depends on the pie, he wrote.

He hit Send. Her message came back right away.

Apple, pumpkin, pecan, ice cream. Deliciousness guaranteed.

Yes, please.

All of the above?

Yes.

Four o'clock sharp. Earlier if you want to.

Thank you.

My dad wants to meet you.

Does he think we're dating?

Noooooo! Just football stuff.

Okay.

Four.

He muted his phone and put it back on the coffee table. He closed his eyes.

Near sleep, he thought of the package from Emporia State. He thought of Coach Steve telling him he needed a plan. He had never thought of making a plan before. At least not solidly, at least not so you could write it down or discuss it as though it were a real thing. An actual path. Hawny might join the Marines. Hawny would like that. Once or twice they had talked about enlisting as buddies—some branches of the military let you do that—but Zeb wasn't sure he would like someone ordering him around. He had too much of Uncle Pushee's influence in his blood to accept that. But if he didn't go into the military, what was he going to do? That was what Coach Steve wanted him to think about.

THURSDAY 6

"You can come to the restaurant if you like . . . it's Thanksgiving, Zeb, and you should eat something proper. You can bring Hawny if you want to. Hawny, you're more than welcome."

"I'm all set, Mrs. Holloway," Hawny said, his fingers banging the video-game console. He didn't look back at her; he kept his eyes on the television. Now and then Zeb heard the sounds of his mother getting dressed. "We're heading over to my cousin's in Vermont."

"Well, then, Zeb, I don't want you to be alone on Thanksgiving Day! What's Uncle Pushee doing? Have you asked him?"

She came over and stood beside the television.

"He didn't say," Zeb said, defending Hawny's man in NBA Jam. He didn't look up at his mom. Looking up only made her more insistent.

"Zeb, listen to me! I don't want you staying here and eating a pizza. You can come down to the restaurant and eat a decent meal. Lorelei won't mind. She's grateful to have me working on Thanksgiving."

"I'm fine, honest, Mom. I have a place to go. I've been invited to dinner."

"Where?"

Zeb shrugged. He didn't want to get into it with her in front of Hawny.

But Hawny had the same question.

"Where?" he asked.

"Ferron Ellis asked me over."

"Ferron Ellis?" Hawny asked. "The girl from the ice cream shop?"

"Isn't that a girl from your class . . ."

"From Mrs. Shapiro's second grade," Zeb answered. "She moved away and now she's back. She invited me for dinner."

"My man!" Hawny said and jammed his shoulder into Zeb's. "The women will not leave this man alone, Mrs. Holloway. QB! He's got QB sauce going on!"

"Good. That's fine. I remember her, I think. Cute little thing."

"She was fat then," Zeb said. "Now she's not."

"That's rude, Zeb."

"I didn't mean it that way. I meant it as a way to identify her for you. You know, so you can remember her. Now can we get back to playing, Mom? Please?"

She didn't move from in front of the video game, though.

"You give me your word you're having Thanksgiving at her house, right? If I come home and find you here, I'll be heartbroken, I swear, Zeb. You're playing straight with me, right?"

"Yes, Mom. I promise."

Zeb felt his mother's lips on his cheek suddenly. Then he watched her kiss Hawny too.

"You're good boys. Both of you. I mean it. You're nice boys."

"Thanks, Mrs. Holloway."

"Okay, I'm out of here. Zeb, I'll see you around nine or so. It might run late. And tomorrow is going to be another full day. Do you have practice?"

"Yes."

"Okay, fill the stove before you go. I hate coming home to a cold house."

"I'll make sure he fills it, Mrs. Holloway."

"Thanks, Hawny. Hawny, you know you're a bit of a suck-up, don't you?"

Hawny laughed hard at that. Zeb held up his finger to pause everything while his mother cleared out of the camper. He identified her sounds as she left: coat, keys, purse, door, shoes on steps, car door, keys, ignition, radio, tire sounds, pause, merge onto 25 South, acceleration, quiet. He hated to admit it, but it was a relief to have her gone.

"Ferron Ellis?" Hawny asked, picking up his controller. "What the hell? I thought you were playing the Stella card."

"It was weird with her. I couldn't get T.T. out of my mind."

"Eating another man's supper, dude!"

"Shut up, Hawny."

"It is what it is. T.T. is gone and good riddance. I never liked the jerk."

"He was something else on the field. That's the whole reason we're in the championship game."

"I know. Everyone knows that. That doesn't mean you can't come in and do your thing. You throw better than he ever did."

"Maybe. Maybe not. Jimbo has the freaking arm. He can lay it out."

"Yeah, but he's got the brains of a dragonfly. Coach K knows that, you know? This whole shebang is on your shoulders."

"Way to help me with the pressure."

"You feeling pressure?"

"Well, what do you think? I'm suddenly playing in the state championship game. It's the biggest thing around here right now. I have no idea if I can do okay. I think I can, but I don't know."

"You can do it."

"Depends if I feel it in my heart or my balls."

Hawny looked at him. "You can do it, Zeb. I don't know why I know it, but I do. All you've ever needed was a chance."

"Thanks, Hawny."

"It's true, though."

"It's just calming it all down. That's what I need to do. I need to get into that place you go to right before you pull the trigger on a good deer. That's what I keep thinking."

"A lot of people are pulling for you, Zeb. Whether you know it or not, people are pulling for you. They never liked T.T. much, but they like you. Trouble is, you're slow as shit and run all hunched over like a gorilla. No, no, kidding. People want you to do okay. Honest."

Hawny picked up the console. He resumed the game and started running his players down the court.

"So did she ask you?"

"Who?"

"Ferron, that's who, ass-hat."

"She said to come by for some dinner. No big deal."

Hawny stole the ball from Zeb's team and ran it back the other way. Zeb covered the man with the ball, but that player passed it off for an easy lay-up. Zeb put the console down. He didn't feel like playing. He wanted a nap. He wanted to be alone, although he couldn't say why. He wondered if he had to wear anything special to Ferron's house. He didn't imagine so. Just jeans and a clean shirt or something. That would probably be enough.

"You done? You admit I kicked your ass?" Hawny asked.

"I need a nap."

"I should get going anyway. It's a two-hour drive to my cousin's and now we have snow to deal with."

"Just a little snow."

"Pushee and Whoopie probably have boners with this snow. They can track a deer anytime they like."

"They were going out today."

"They are hard core. You know I once asked Whoopie about deer hunting as a boy and he said he was almost sixteen before he realized there was a season for deer. He just grew up taking one whenever he liked. You think we'll be like them someday? Just farting around and hunting deer?"

"I don't know," Zeb said. "Right now, I just wish my knee felt better."

"Is it bad?"

Zeb shrugged. "I'll keep resting it. It should be okay."

"I'd give you a ride over to Ferron's but it's too early, right?"

"I'll figure something out."

"Don't walk on your leg, man."

"I won't."

"I had you down for Stella, Zebulon, you old dog. I figured you and T.T. would be Eskimo brothers."

"Shut it, Hawny."

Hawny punched him on the shoulder and then shot to his feet. Zeb couldn't move that fast even if he wanted to. His shin felt stiff and hollow, like a bird leg. Hawny held out his fist and knuckle-bumped him.

"Happy Thanksgiving, man."

"You too."

"State."

"State."

Whoopie dropped him off at Ferron's house. It was a big white house on a big white lawn. Snow covered the front of the house and the bushes and the wood chips in the garden. Someone had been out with a push broom to whisk off the front walk, and the broom now leaned casually against a support post on the porch. The house looked the way a house was supposed to look on Thanksgiving. It looked better, really, Zeb thought. And the broom looked like a man who had stepped out to have a breath and leaned against the post to watch the snow. Seeing things like that, Zeb knew, meant he was nervous.

The only thing that didn't look quite right was Whoopie's truck, the old Dodge with rusted-out mud panels and a dented front fender. Zeb had almost asked to be dropped off a block short, but he couldn't do that to Whoopie.

"Thanks," Zeb said when Whoopie stopped in front of the house. "Thanks for the ride."

"Don't mention it. Nice house. I know these people," Whoopie said, bending down to get a better view through the side window. "Ellises, right?"

"Right."

"I knew Old Man Ellis, must be thirty years back. Hell yes, I know them. Nice family. The old man made his money in the shoe business down in Manchester or Laconia. Laconia, I think. You're running with the right people, Zebulon."

"I'm not running with anyone. I'm just going to dinner."

"Going to dinner is running with people. Anytime you pick up a fork with people, you're running with them."

Zeb opened his door and slid out. His knee felt a little better.

"Happy Thanksgiving," Zeb said.

"You too. Good luck on Saturday if I don't see you."

"Thanks, Whoopie."

"Your uncle Pushee is pretty proud of you, even if he doesn't say it. He'd pop a button on his vest if he wasn't such a hard-hearted old bastard."

Zeb felt something inflate in his heart and head and he had to stand still for a second before he answered.

"He has a funny way of showing it," he managed.

"Someday I'll tell you all about your uncle Pushee, but today isn't that day."

"Thanks again."

"You'll do great. You've done a lot just to get on that field, son. For what it's worth, I'm proud of you too."

Zeb nodded and closed the door. He watched Whoopie's truck rattle off down the road. He squared his shoulders and walked deliberately to the door. He sent his mind down to his knee to feel it. It felt better, but not 100 percent. It felt like a book page that had been turned down for too long, then had trouble regaining its shape.

He patted down his hair, checked his fly, then rang the doorbell. It made a bonging sound deep in the house. A second later the door swung open. A little girl, maybe five, stood with the door against her shoulder. She didn't say anything. She didn't ask him what he wanted or point him inside. He didn't know quite what to do.

"Is Ferron here?" he asked. "I'm a friend of Ferron's."

The little girl nodded. She had dark food stains on the front of her dress. Behind her, the house obviously held many people. Zeb heard voices and music and something like a television running under everything.

"Who is it, Macy?" a woman's voice called. "Don't hold the door open. You're making the house cold."

The girl—Macy, Zeb assumed—opened the door wider. He stepped inside. He couldn't help smiling at the girl as she swung the door shut behind him. The house smelled like all the best things in the world.

"Oh, hi," a woman said, passing by him with a plate of cranberries and a bottle of wine tucked into the crook of her arm. She was tall and thin and wore a blue dress and black heels. Zeb realized he'd probably underdressed. "Are you Ferron's friend? I'm Eleanor, Ferron's stepmom."

"Yes, ma'am. I'm Zeb."

"Macy," the woman carefully instructed the little girl while her hands arranged things on the wide dining-room table, "take Zeb into the kitchen and find Ferron. She's in there somewhere.

And tell people they should get ready to eat. And please tell them to turn off the football . . . now."

Macy nodded. Zeb followed her. The little girl dodged quickly around corners and Zeb became aware of people taking notice of him. He deliberately kept his eyes on Macy. The smell of roasting food grew stronger the deeper they went into the house. They passed a staircase where a pyramid of little children sat, playing something, all of them chattering like crows. They passed an old dog stretched out on his dog bed. Written on the dog bed was *Heigh-Ho Silver.* The dog thumped his tail twice.

Macy pushed open a swinging door at the end of the hallway and suddenly Zeb found himself in a big, bright kitchen with an enormous island in the center. It had a granite top; a huge bowl of apples stood in the middle, their skins so red they looked nearly purple. A roasted turkey, at least thirty pounds, probably larger, Zeb judged, cooled on the table beside the apples. It looked to be done perfectly. A woman who strongly resembled Eleanor sat at one end of the island sipping wine. A man with gray hair pulled back in a short ponytail stirred something at the stove. He looked intensely at what he was doing. Zeb tried to imagine his place in this scene, but before he could do anything, Macy ran around the island and went to a girl standing at the sink. It was Ferron. Macy tugged at her skirt and Ferron turned around. She looked down at Macy, and Macy pointed to Zeb. Ferron looked over at him and her eyes went into his. She smiled. Her whole face smiled.

"I'm so glad you came!" she said when she'd made it past Macy and stood in front of him. She went up on her toes and kissed him on the cheek. The kiss surprised him.

"Daddy, this is Zeb," she said, putting her arm through Zeb's arm. She turned him slightly so the man at the stove could see him. Her dad looked him up and down.

"Don't suppose you can carve a turkey?" her dad asked. "My nitwit brother, Henry, is here and he always hacks the thing to death. Ferron said you're a hunter."

Zeb still hadn't recovered from the kiss. Ferron's arm through his felt as perfect as the house.

"I can carve," Zeb said.

"Can you really carve or are you just saying it?"

"I've cleaned a lot of birds for my uncle."

"George Pushee, right? Yep. I knew George years ago. Ferron, will you set him up with the knife and everything? Make it look pretty, you two. A lot of work went into that bird. Maybe just carve one side and we'll leave the other for show."

Her father moved back to the stove, then turned around.

"Nice to meet you, Zeb. Sorry. Under a little pressure right now."

"Nice to meet you too, sir."

Ferron squeezed his arm against her. He felt blood go to his face and neck.

"I didn't tell you you'd have to work for your supper, did I?" Ferron whispered. "I'm really glad you're here, Zeb."

"Glad to be here."

"Want to wash your hands quick? That's my aunt Eliza," Ferron said, pointing to the woman at the end of the island. "Be careful of her. She's the wicked sister."

"Hi, Zeb," Eliza said. "You two look cute together. Adorable, really."

This time Zeb saw Ferron blush. She dropped his arm and went to get him set up. He moved to the sink and washed his hands with dish soap. Under most circumstances, he would have been dead nervous, but he knew how to carve. That was something he could do better than most people. That was something people on Redtree Road could do with their eyes closed.

"I've got an electric carving knife," Ferron's dad said, his face toward the stove, his voice loud enough to carry. "Some people hate them, but they're hard to beat on a turkey . . . Ferron, give him a choice. We have the good carving set from your grandfather. Macy, please move out of the kitchen, sweetheart. I'm going to trip over you. Get everyone moving toward the table. That can be your job. Now scoot."

Zeb dried his hands on a paper towel and stood with Ferron in front of the turkey. She had an electric carving knife in one hand and a book of knives already on the table. He took the electric knife and flicked it on and off. It made a sharp, busy sound like a hedge clipper. Ferron, he decided, smelled like a garden. He wanted her arm back through his.

He took a large fork from the carving set and began slicing the turkey. He made a cut horizontally so the slices would fall forward, as properly carved turkey should. The electric knife made it simple.

"I knew you'd be good at this," Ferron said. "That's beautiful. The best we've had."

"I don't know about that."

"Dad, are you seeing this?"

Suddenly Zeb felt Mr. Ellis near his shoulder. Mr. Ellis put his hand on Zeb's upper arm.

"You are hereby invited to Thanksgiving dinner every year for the rest of your life as long as you carve the turkey," Mr. Ellis said and went back to the stove. Eliza, Zeb noticed, had gone to ferry things into the dining room. Zeb heard people moving toward dinner and the television had gone off.

"I have a present for you," Ferron said. "A surprise."

"What kind of surprise?"

Ferron went to the refrigerator and returned with a bottle of Fanta orange soda. She put it beside the turkey. He looked at her, not comprehending.

"In second grade, in Mrs. Shapiro's class, you said you loved Fanta orange soda. Do you remember?"

"I don't really remember," Zeb admitted.

"Well, you said it, so when I saw it in the store . . ."

He looked down at the turkey. He felt choked and silly. Nobody had ever remembered a thing like that about him. Not in his whole life.

"Thank you," he said.

"It's just a goofy thing. You don't have to drink it."

She put her arm through his again. He looked at her. She had the kindest eyes he had ever seen.

He sat next to her. That made it hard to eat or talk, but he did his best. Her dad had put on music—nice, soft swing piano music—that played loud enough to obscure any awkward moments.

Macy and five other children sat at a table closer to the kitchen. They couldn't be persuaded to remain at the children's table. They approached the larger table like pirates, each one trying a new tactic to win a place. Uncle Pushee would have tolerated that for about two seconds, Zeb reflected. Kids in his house would have known the seas were safer away from the table.

"So, Zeb," Mr. Ellis said at one point after the plates had been passed once around the adult table, "you're playing for the state championship on Saturday? I read about it in the paper. I haven't been following it closely, I'll admit."

"Yes, sir."

"That's wonderful," Eleanor said. "You must be very excited."

"Of course he's excited," Henry, Mr. Ellis's brother, said, "they're playing for the state championship."

"I read about this fellow T.T.," Mr. Ellis said, sipping his wine and then pointing to Zeb with the rim of his glass. "Was he as good as they say? They said he was the best player Rumney ever saw. Is that true?"

"He was one of the top recruits in the country. USC wanted him," Zeb said.

"Shoes to fill," Henry said. "Mighty big ones."

"How do you think the team will do?" Eliza asked. "Are you feeling confident?"

"We'll do pretty well, I think. Hard to say. We've had some good practices leading up to the game. We're spreading the offense out a little because of their defense. They have a great defense."

"You practice tomorrow, don't you?" Ferron asked.

She sat close to him. She sat close enough that she seemed to breathe his air.

"We have a morning practice. Coach K wants us to get used to playing at game time. He doesn't leave much to chance. Anyway, this food is delicious," Zeb said, trying to change the subject. He didn't want to be the center of attention. Eliza asked for the creamed onions and Zeb passed them down to Ferron. "It's really great."

A half hour later, Zeb stood outside in the backyard with Ferron. He felt heavy and full from the meal, but happy too. The knee felt okay. Another glancing hit would knock it down for good, but he could live with the pain. He had to live with it. That was just the way it was.

"I've got something for us to do," Ferron said. "Are you freezing?"

"No, not at all."

"If you get cold, tell me. But I have this thing I do . . ."

"What thing?"

Ferron said to follow her onto the backyard lawn. When they reached the section closest to the house, she put out her hand like a safety patrol person keeping a child from crossing the street.

"Sometimes I do more sophisticated pictures . . . but tonight I thought we could make something simple."

"How do you mean?"

"We just make lines by shuffling our feet in the snow. I've drawn some pretty good stuff out in Arizona, in sand. I'll show you sometime."

"So what do you want to make?"

"Let's make a circle inside a box. That's an easy one. You go that way, and I'll go this way. We'll meet at the top. Try to keep the lines straight and square off the edges. Then we'll make the circle."

"I'm not sure I get it."

"It's just a circle in a square. It's like a crop circle," she said in a low voice. "Just a design in a large space."

Ferron started walking. She walked like a small train, shuffling her feet as she went. Zeb watched her for a second, then took off in the other direction. He felt cold, but not too cold. He didn't relish the thought of walking home. He stopped and checked on Ferron. She had already gone around the first corner at the bottom of the rectangle. He picked it up. He had almost caught up with her by the time they reached the center on the top of the picture.

"Perfect," she said as they came together. "Now comes the tricky part."

Zeb knew he would remember whatever it was they were doing out here, just as he would remember the dinner and the Fanta soda and her arm through his.

She took off on a parabola inside the rectangle and he tried his best to form the other side of it. A half a dozen times, she laughed and yelled to him to go slow, take it easy.

When they met at the bottom she made them hook arms and do a slow do-si-do to put a ribbon on the picture. She held his hand and led him up to the deck, retracing their steps so they wouldn't spoil the effect.

Zeb noticed she didn't drop his hand. He noticed he didn't drop hers either. He stood beside her and looked out at the wintry yard. They had made a lopsided circle in a box.

He kissed her again.

"Don't forget your food," she whispered. "I have to get back."

She kissed him. Zeb sat in the passenger seat of her Volvo

station wagon. The seats were heated. She kept the moonroof open a smidge so that they had air but not noise. He couldn't count how many times they had kissed. Fifty, maybe. Maybe a hundred. He had never felt anything like it.

"Thank you for having me to dinner. It meant a lot. My family's not great about holidays."

"Everyone loved you. They all think you're really polite."

"I try to be. My mom's training. It's habit now."

"Dad wants to go to the game on Saturday, but I told him it was over in Durham."

"It's just a game."

"Well, we both know that isn't quite true," she said and kissed him again. "It's not just a game. It's the state championship game."

They did not hug. They didn't do anything except let their lips touch over and over. It felt perfect. They hadn't even removed their seat belts. Zeb knew they had both decided to be careful. That was the only way it all made sense.

"Do you have your Fanta?" she asked, pulling back to square behind the steering wheel.

"I do."

Part of him wanted her to go. Part of him didn't want her to think too much about where he lived. He hadn't said he lived in the camper. He let her think he lived in Uncle Pushee's house. That wasn't a lie, exactly, but it also wasn't exactly the truth.

"I've liked you a long time, Zeb. I had a crush on you when we were little. I thought I should be honest about that."

"Seriously?"

She nodded.

"I knew we weren't finished with each other. I knew it the minute I saw you with Stella."

"You're amazing."

"I have to go. Otherwise my dad will think we're having a mad make-out session."

"We are."

He leaned over and kissed her, then popped his door open. He pulled the leftovers out and his bottle of orange Fanta.

He got out of the car and purposely did not walk toward the camper or the house. He stood in the driveway and waved. She backed up and turned around. Her car drifted away in the glossy wetness of the snow.

Coach K once yanked my brother off a motorbike when he took it around the running track.

Deserved it.

Not really. Who made Coach K king of the world?

Your brother shouldn't have been on it.

The track or the bike?

Either.

Screw Coach K.

Mr. Television followed Zeb into the Quonset hut, squeezing through as soon as the door opened. Zeb wasn't sure if Uncle Pushee was in the shop, but it was worth checking. His truck was in the driveway and the absence of tire tracks suggested he hadn't gone out. Uncle Pushee preferred the shop to his house in most ways. He claimed the house was haunted.

Zeb put the leftovers on the worktable and shook out some kibble for Mr. Television. The cat humped his back under Zeb's hand. Zeb stroked him for a minute or two. "Where's Uncle Pushee?" he whispered, but the cat simply swirled under his hand until the food fell into the bowl. Then Mr. Television crouched slightly and began eating.

Uncle Pushee hadn't turned on the lights. Zeb flicked on the overhead and he saw Uncle Pushee almost at once. He was asleep inside a maroon Ford F-250 truck that he had in for bodywork. Zeb couldn't know for sure, but he guessed he had been drinking. He walked over and tapped lightly on the glass beside Uncle Pushee's head. He had to tap several times to wake him. Uncle Pushee jolted a little, turned to look at him, then ran his hand over his face. Sometimes Zeb could see a glimmer of himself in Uncle Pushee's features, but not tonight.

"I brought you some food," Zeb said softly. "Thought you might like some Thanksgiving dinner."

Uncle Pushee nodded. He opened the door and slid his feet out. He was unsteady when he moved his butt off the car seat. He staggered a twitch, and Zeb supported him with his hand.

"Have a nice dinner?" Uncle Pushee asked, tottering toward the stool by the workbench. He grew steadier as he walked.

"Great food."

"What do you have for me?"

"Most of the fixings. Turkey and stuffing . . . some mashed potatoes and sweet potatoes. Let me warm them up. Creamed onions too. You like those."

Zeb carried the dish to the shop microwave. He hated to put

the food in the filthy microwave, but he knew he couldn't have Uncle Pushee wait long for his supper. He warmed it for two minutes and washed a dirty dish and some silverware in the sink. He dried everything in the time it took for the microwave to finish, then he slipped into a pair of welding gloves and carried the hot dish to his uncle.

"Careful, it's hot."

"Wow, that's a proper supper."

"Happy Thanksgiving."

Uncle Pushee nodded. The food looked great and smelled even better. Uncle Pushee ate with his head down; still drunk, Zeb imagined. Zeb pulled a seat over beside his uncle. It felt funny to watch his uncle eat such a carefully prepared meal under the harsh shop light. For a moment, for a reason he couldn't fully identify, he felt a painful fondness for his uncle. He was a hard-working man who did his best and now he was drunk on Thanksgiving, lonely, eating a meal with his dirty hands under a fluorescent light. Zeb felt mixed up watching him. He wished for a thing to say, a string of conversation he could employ, to bring his uncle some pleasure or happiness. His drunkenness could be a thin line, though. On the other side of the merry drunk, Uncle Pushee had a field of brambles. It was hard to know when you were leaving one space to go to the next.

"How is it?" Zeb asked after a few minutes.

"Finest kind."

"Good. I'm glad you like it."

"Nice of them to send it over."

"They were glad to do it."

"They still live in that big white house? I did some foundation work on that house years and years ago. Dug out the sills and replaced them. We had that house on jacks most of the summer."

"Was that with your dad?"

Uncle Pushee nodded. "Never was a man better around a foundation than your grandfather."

"Did my dad work with you?"

His uncle nodded again. "Lawrence was a lazy ass, though. You sent him down to the lumberyard for a two-by-four and you might as well have sent him to Arabia. That's how some people are."

"You said he was pretty good when he set his mind to it. My dad, I mean."

"Oh, he had a hand for it. No question about that. The ladies liked talking to him because he could see what they wanted. You take him into a kitchen and get him talking to the lady of the house, and a kitchen renovation was as good as signed and sealed. Your grandfather could never believe it, but it was easy as pie for Lawrence."

"So he was kind of good at sales."

Uncle Pushee shrugged.

"If that's what you want to call it."

"You think we'll ever hear from him again, Uncle Pushee?"

"Lawrence?"

Zeb nodded. It was like moving up on a deer. Zeb didn't want to startle him or say the wrong thing.

"I understand your need to ask, but we'll only see Lawrence again if he's in trouble. He might be dead, for all we know. I'm not saying that to hurt you, Zeb, it's just his makeup. Some people like to be at home and some people don't. Your father couldn't sit still. Half the world's problems come from people who can't sit still."

"He was in Oregon last you heard from him?"

"Must be ten years now."

"Do you think he felt bad for leaving Mom and me?"

Uncle Pushee shrugged.

"He doesn't have that kind of bone inside him. He's not made that way."

"Mom says he was narcissistic."

"You mean self-important?"

"I guess."

"Selfish, really. You couldn't blame him for it. That was his makeup. Your mom saw it too late. We all knew it, but she couldn't see it. Walked into the lion's den when you get right down to it. She didn't stand a chance of holding him. Of course she wouldn't have listened. Young people have to make their own mistakes. The world would be a calmer place if young people could learn from what older people know. But it's our fate to make our own mistakes."

Uncle Pushee stood and carried his empty plate to the sink. He picked out a last piece of turkey and put it on Mr. Television's bowl. The cat had already gone to sleep near the wood stove. On his way back, Uncle Pushee picked up the orange Fanta and held it up to ask if he could have it. Zeb nodded. Uncle Pushee dug his penknife out of his pocket and popped the top off the bottle. He took a long drink.

"I'm turning in," he said, smothering a gassy burp. "You tell those people thanks for that dinner. That was very nice. Set me up just fine."

"I will, Uncle Pushee."

"Your dad wasn't a bad man, Zeb. He just wasn't cut out for this kind of life. Sometimes I think he made the right decision. Not about you and your mom, but about clearing out of here. Not much opportunity in this neck of the woods."

"You ever think about moving?"

"Only every day."

He laughed and began turning off lights. When they went out the door, the only thing Zeb could see inside was the reflection of Mr. Television's eyes staring into the darkness. Uncle Pushee trudged one way to his house and Zeb climbed into the camper and closed the door. His knee hurt, but it was bearable.

Ferron's text came in around eleven.

It was a photo, taken from the upstairs window at her house, of the yard diagram they had made in the snow. Only she had gone back out and worked on it. Now instead of merely a circle in a box, she had illustrated an entire scene. The circle had turned into a clock with hands and numbers, all cleverly linked, and she had completed a sort of filigree in the four corners of the picture frame.

She wrote in block letters on the left side: *Zeb comes to dinner.*

On the other side she wrote: *Thanksgiving 2017.*

The clock hands stood at four o'clock.

He had to squint to see the words. He studied the design a long time. He liked thinking of her out there, maybe thinking of him.

Awesome, he texted. *You're awesome.*

Did you see the others?

He went back to the link. He hadn't seen at first that her

drawing of the clock was only the last of dozens of snow photos. She had also done designs in sand at the beach and in what looked to be a meadow on the side of a hill. She had cut the grass into a lightning bolt with stars flashing off one side. In the sand at the beach, she had drawn a Labrador with a ball in its mouth running toward the water.

Blown away, he wrote, and he was.

I'm arty. Or nuts. You pick.

I pick you. I want to see you tomorrow.

When?

After practice? Afternoon?

Yes, please.

I'll text. Probably around two or so.

Sleep tight.

He couldn't sleep afterward. He thought of Ferron and of Uncle Pushee and of his mom coming in with her sore feet and tired body, and he wondered where his father was right at that moment. He didn't believe his father had died. He thought he probably would have heard something like that if it had occurred.

Then for a while he went through the plays he would perform on Saturday. He tried to visualize the game. The game had grown bigger, not only in his mind, but all over the town. The boosters had hung banners from two more telephone wires, each one exhorting them to beat Merrymeeting. Tomorrow night, the local public television station planned to host a call-in show to discuss the game. Coach K would field questions. Zeb understood his role in the game would be a major topic. He wasn't sure he wanted to watch. He also wasn't sure he could resist.

Near sleep, he thought again of what Coach Steve had said. He needed a plan for his life. Spring would come and people would begin to move. Winter froze everyone in place, it seemed to him, but in spring things cracked and thawed and began shifting. People moved away, or took new jobs, or ended long-term relationships. Spring brought things back to life and that meant you had been partially dead for a while. He understood something in him had begun to wake. He sensed it. He couldn't have put it back to sleep even if he'd wanted to.

FRIDAY 7

"How does that feel?" Mrs. Gilmore asked. "Does it restrict things a lot?"

Zeb flexed his knee softly. It didn't have much movement.

"Don't baby it; ease into it. Take your time. You can get up and move it if that feels better."

Zeb climbed off the training table. Dino stood beside Mrs. Gilmore. They had discussed sending Zeb to an orthopedic surgeon to see if he needed to have the knee drained. They had talked as if he were a cut of ham, or a quartered deer. They were kind otherwise, bringing him ice water and making sure he didn't suffer too much as they taped the knee and stretched an elastic bandage around it. Three boosters stood beside the window looking out, their attention turning sometimes to him and sometimes to the start of practice forming outside the window.

"Feels pretty good," Zeb said, bending the knee and then trying his weight on it. It felt better but still not great.

"You're going to have to judge what you can do," Mrs. Gilmore said, standing back to appraise her work. "I don't think you'll damage anything by playing. I wouldn't let you play if I thought that. But it's still got a good deal of fluid on it. I'm not sure why it didn't settle more yesterday."

"I stayed off it as much as I could."

She nodded. He didn't know if she believed him.

"You only have to get through one game," Dino said. "That's something."

"Championship game," one of the boosters said.

He wore a yellow slicker and a rain hat. It had been raining and sleeting for most of the morning. The snow had already disappeared, washed away overnight. Zeb thought of Ferron's snow drawing fading to nothing in her backyard.

"Thank you," Zeb said to Mrs. Gilmore. "I think it should be fine."

"Don't push it today," she answered. "Tomorrow's the day."

"Yes, ma'am."

"Dino, you going out?" Mrs. Gilmore asked. "Walk Zeb out. Make sure the bandage feels okay, will you?"

Dino nodded. Zeb went gingerly down the stairs of the field house. The rest of the team had already gone out to practice. Zeb finished dressing quickly. By now it felt like the oldest routine imaginable. Shoulder pads, pants, jersey, pull-down, socks, cleats, helmet, mouthpiece. He could have dressed in the dark. His jersey felt damp already.

He walked carefully on the concrete floor, then broke into a light trot once he gained the dirt field. Zeb used the fifty yards between the locker room and the scrimmage line to test his leg. He found he had to keep it stiff, mostly, although somewhere inside the flex he found some movement. He didn't feel clear on what his knee could or couldn't do. Mrs. Gilmore didn't know and neither did he. He thought quickly of T.T., how things would have been entirely different if T.T. had been healthy for the championship game. Even on one leg, T.T. would have posed a threat to the opposing team.

Hawny jogged over and ran the last twenty yards with him. Hawny didn't give a damn anymore about what he should or shouldn't do on the practice field. Zeb understood that. It was Hawny's last day on the nut squad.

"How's it feel?" Hawny asked. "Looks like you can run on it."

"It feels weird."

"Jimbo is running first team, but he doesn't know what he's doing."

Even as he said that, a few players began pounding their fists on their thigh pads in greeting. It took Zeb a moment to realize they were greeting him. Somebody chanted, "QB," and then others followed. It went "QB," thigh-pad hit, "QB," thigh-pad hit.

Coach K took a few steps away from the practice and met Zeb before he reached the full squad. Hawny jogged back to the nut squad. Coach K put his arm around Zeb's shoulders and made a motion with his other hand to get the team focused back on practice.

"How's it feeling, Zeb?" Coach K asked softly. "You seem to move okay. Not too bad, is it?"

"I think it's fine."

"I need to know what you can do, Zeb. Give me the straight low-down. Can you run on it?"

"Maybe eighty percent. I don't know yet."

"Well, the big thing will be to see how you can do moving to run our plays. That's going to be the key. And see if you can plant to throw. That's your back leg. That's your foundation."

"Yes, sir."

"Jimbo is doing the best he can, but we're going to need you, Zeb. You're our guy tomorrow, hear? You're starting and playing as long as you can. Jimbo has a couple specialty plays, but you're the main cog."

"Yes, sir."

"Okay, stretch out and then we'll see how you do. Go easy. Save something for tomorrow."

"Yes, sir."

"Confidence, remember. Showing the team confidence is half the battle. That's what a quarterback has to do, right?"

Coach K lifted his arm off Zeb's shoulders. Zeb took a few minutes to stretch. Then he called Hawny over and played catch with him. Sleet came down harder. Despite the fact that the championship game was scheduled for the next day, Zeb felt the team had grown tired and stale. Maybe Thanksgiving had made them lazy. That combined with the weather gave the practice a sense of dull routine. The season was over, really. Win or lose the next day, the season ended tomorrow.

"All right, first-team O," Coach Hoch called. "Let's run our first series for state. Let's be crisp, people. Time to put up or shut up. We'll put it all on the line now. Not holding anything back."

Zeb underhanded the ball to Hawny, then trotted into the huddle.

For the first time since T.T. had gone down, Zeb felt he belonged in the huddle. He looked around at his teammates. They needed him now and they knew it. Jimbo wasn't the answer. If they wanted to beat Merrymeeting, they had to put their confidence in him. It was as simple as that and Zeb felt something click inside him, something strong and even and quick. He called a boom play, a simple handoff to Otzman. He watched Otzman nod. McCay, the right guard, nodded too.

"On two," Zeb said. "Ready, break."

They all clapped together and it was like a bright rifle shot. Zeb walked quietly after the squad, his eyes checking where the defense would line up the next day, his body feeling good at last. He ignored his knee as much as he could. He bent down and called the cadence, his hands under Jiler's broad butt. When the ball popped into his palms, he spun easily and slapped it into Otzman's belly. Otzman stabbed through the line and kept going twenty yards in a full sprint, his legs churning, the sleet turning him into something wild and primitive, a horse running to shake a snake from his legs.

It was a tradition for the underclassmen to carry the seniors off the field on the last day of practice. The sleet came down so hard Zeb wasn't sure they would bother with the ritual, but when Coach K called them all together at last, everyone looked around, happy-eyed, and Coach Steve swatted anyone nearby.

"That's it, boys. That's the last practice of the season . . . pretty miserable day today, but they're calling for good weather tomorrow," Coach K said, his ball cap dripping from the brim. "Before we go in, on a serious note . . . I want to thank you all for sticking with us. You're a great group of young men and we—the coaches and I—we want to thank you for letting us work with you this season. We have had a great year, but it's not over yet. But thank you. Today is a day to say thanks. It's been an honor."

That brought a hoot of appreciation. Everyone waited on a knee. The sleet wouldn't stop and wouldn't give a person a chance to get a breath. Zeb didn't kneel; he didn't want his knee on the cold ground. The sleet had dripped into his ribs and heart, and chill radiated out from his core. The knee felt decent. He had run the plays he needed to run but then had stepped out to let Jimbo work on some of his timing. Zeb felt a degree of fatalism slip into his thinking. Whatever was going to happen was going to happen. He felt himself almost letting go. It was like squeezing off a shot in a dense thicket. The bullet might go through uninfluenced by a random twig or it might not. Fate had something to do with it.

"Now . . . the bus is leaving here at eight fifteen sharp tomorrow morning," Coach K continued. "Breakfast at seven thirty in the high school cafeteria. Usual routines, that's all. Dino will help, but check your gear tonight and tomorrow. Durham should be pretty crowded. The stands are big . . . don't get distracted. It's just a football field. You've been playing on the same size fields all year. Are there any questions?"

"My parents want to know about the booster buses. Do they leave at the same time?" someone asked. Zeb couldn't see who it was. The helmets and the sleet made it difficult to distinguish one person from another.

"Coach Hoch?" Coach K asked. "That's your bailiwick."

"Same time as ours. Eight fifteen sharp. We'll make a little flotilla going over. They need to bring a printout of their tickets. Make sure you tell them that. They won't be let on the buses without it."

"Leaving from the cafeteria or from here?"

Coach Hoch looked uncertain.

"From here," he answered finally.

"Seniors, line up," Coach Steve yelled. "Let's do this!"

The coaches formed a line and the seniors walked down and shook hands with them. Simple, Zeb thought. A week before, though, Zeb wouldn't have meant much to anyone here. Now as he went down the line, the coaches shook his hand firmly and gave him a little juice. Hawny went down two spots ahead of him. When Hawny finished, he jumped on the backs of two sophomores, Deombleg and Johnson, then made them form a seat for him to ride out in style. He sat like a king as they carried him off. They had been on the nut squad with him. Hawny blew kisses at anyone who looked. It made everyone laugh.

Zeb passed on the ride offered by the freshman QB. Zeb didn't trust his knee. He didn't want to hit it or get it jostled at this point. He walked beside Coach Steve to the locker room. Sleet had turned everything white and gray.

"How are you feeling, Zeb?" Coach Steve asked, his hand spread on Zeb's lower back. "You solid about tomorrow?"

"Yes, sir, I think so."

"It's a funny thing. It's just a game and it's also more than a game. Keep it in perspective, though. Ask yourself who won the Super Bowl or World Series three years ago. You forget, probably. We all forget. Enjoy the game, that's the thing."

"Yes, sir."

"You're going to play great, I think. I have a feeling about it. We may use Jimbo for a down or two, but this is your game. It's going to be your day."

"I'll do my best."

"I know you will. We all know that. The coaches have confidence in you, Zeb. More than you might know."

Coach Hoch called Coach Steve away then. Coach Steve trotted off, jazzing around with the trailing players and laughing at the piggybacks. Zeb walked off the field alone. He wanted to do something meaningful, maybe take a last look around, but the sleet drove him inside.

In the locker room, Hawny had already showered and was sitting on the bench by his locker, a towel wrapped around his waist. He had a cheap cigar in his mouth. The cigar wasn't lit, but he wiggled it up and down, showing off. The two kids who had carried him inside sat on either side of him. Hawny was enjoying himself, Zeb saw.

Zeb walked over and held out his hand. Hawny slapped it, but Zeb kept his hand out. Hawny looked up and to Zeb's surprise he saw his friend had tears in his eyes. The crazy bastard hadn't played a single down in all his time on the team. Not on the varsity. Not even on a kickoff or an extra point. Somehow that made Hawny the purest person on the team and Zeb wanted to acknowledge that. He wanted to pay attention to that, and so when Hawny finally took his hand, Zeb shook it and looked his friend in the eye.

"I admire you, Hawny," he said. "I'm proud of you. You never quit."

"I'm just glad it's over."

"You stuck to it longer than most people would. It's something."

Hawny teared up more. Then he let go of Zeb's hand and turned back to his locker. Zeb wondered if he had said too much or maybe not enough. If T.T. hadn't gone down with an injury, Zeb would have been basically in the same position as Hawny. He would have waited out the season and called it over when the practices ended. He knuckle-bumped the two sophomores and limped over to his locker. His knee felt stiff and cold. It had no warmth in it at all.

Ferron picked him up from practice. Hawny could hardly believe it when Zeb told him he had another ride. He had to repeat it three times. Finally Hawny wiggled his eyebrows and drove off in a flock of vehicles heading over to Friendly's for a late lunch. Try as he might, Zeb could not remember ever having anyone but Hawny give him a ride from practice.

Outise the field house, Zeb texted.

Outise?

Outside.

B rt there.

When she pulled up, he found he couldn't help smiling. He limped around to the passenger side and climbed inside. She had her father's Volvo station wagon. He looked over at her. He smiled again.

"It's good to see you," he said.

"Is it?"

He leaned over and kissed her. She kissed him back. That's just the way it was with her now, he realized. He had no idea how that had happened.

"Maybe this is too fast," she said when he pulled back. "Do you think it's too fast? We should have waited a day to see each other."

"I think you need to get me out of here before the coaches start knocking on our windows."

"Are we doing something illegal?"

"No, they just want our minds on the game."

"I'm a distraction?"

"You are definitely a distraction."

"Good. I've always wanted to be a distraction."

She pulled away from the front of the field house. Something about that felt easy. He took a deep breath and looked at her. She wore a long brown sweater over jeans and had something in her hair—it looked like a tiara—that occasionally caught the afternoon's dull light and flashed it around the interior of the car.

She drove with her hands at nine and three. She did not drive fast.

"I liked your snow painting . . . or footscape . . . or whatever you call it," he said. "Those pictures are something."

"It's just a thing I do. A teacher in eighth grade showed us a film about a Scottish artist who does art outside with sticks and twigs and all sorts of things. That gave me the idea. That's why I do it."

"They're imaginative."

"Do you think so? I never know. They seem so easy sometimes that I don't trust them."

She reached over and took his hand. He curled his fingers over hers.

"You're different," Zeb said.

"Different from other girls? Or different from how I was in second grade?"

"Both, I guess. I don't know. I am having trouble remembering you as a little girl."

"As Tank?"

He tried not to smile, but he couldn't help it. She pulled his hand up to her mouth and bit his knuckles.

"Do you have any idea how obnoxious those boys were about that? I went to bed crying every night!"

"Sorry."

"You do *not* get to be sorry. You get to be penitent. You get to spend your life making up for it. *Sorry* doesn't cut it."

"I am penitent, then."

"Good."

She had said she was bringing him a turkey sandwich, but he had no idea where they were going to eat it. He didn't care. He could have driven beside her for the rest of the day and not minded a bit, but she pulled into the boat launch area near Lake Tarleton. The parking lot stood on a hill overlooking the lake. Only one other car took up a spot in the lot, and it must have belonged to the dog walker who skirted the lake with a Lab by his side.

"I fixed us a picnic," Ferron said. "I thought we could eat it on one of the tables outside, but with the weather, we'll just sit in the car. Maybe we can have a picnic in the back?"

"Okay."

"Are you hungry?"

"You might have made me too nervous to eat."

"Come on," she said as she opened the door and moved around the back of the car. "Let's eat."

He hopped out his side. Sleet continued to spatter the hood and roof of her Volvo. She pushed open the cargo door and it yawned wide. She had folded down the back seats and made a small picnic area with an old sleeping bag for a covering. It took some maneuvering to get his knee to comply as he climbed inside. He had to lean on one elbow to let his knee have room. She sat cross-legged and dug through a wicker picnic basket.

"I hope you are hungry," she said, "because my father prides himself on using up all of the turkey. Every last bit of it. He was delighted you would be eating some more. I don't think anyone ever impressed him as much as you did simply by carving."

"I'm glad to hear that."

"Anyway, he sent over dressing too. And cranberry sauce . . . the gloppy can style, not the real stuff. Do you like that kind?"

He leaned forward and kissed her. He wanted to kiss her every minute, he thought.

"Why are you being so nice to me?" he asked when she pulled back and started yanking out food again. "Is someone paying you or something?"

"Do you think I'm being nice to you?"

"Very nice."

"I think you have a nice deficit. A deficit of niceness. I think more people need to be nice to you. To Zebulon Holloway."

"You can be president of that movement."

"Oh, not president. More like empress."

"Are you wearing a tiara? I couldn't help wondering."

"Do you *think* I'm wearing a tiara?"

"I'm not sure."

"When I run into little girls when I wear it, they don't have to ask. They know."

He smiled.

"So can I ask you something?" she said, arranging his sandwich on a paper plate.

"Sure."

"It's a Stella question. A friend of a friend of a friend said she thought you two were, are, could be, still might be, an item. True or false?"

"False."

"In what way would you say the rumor about you and Stella is false?"

"What does the rumor say?"

"That you were kind . . . of an item, I guess. A thing."

"Far from it, believe me."

"Far from it?"

"Yeah," he said. "We were not an item. We never were. You could say there was some confusion around the time that T.T. left, but that was it."

"Confusion?"

She ate in a circle. He watched her for a second before he accepted the evidence of his eyes. While most people ate a sandwich across, east to west, she circumnavigated the sandwich, taking off a little with each bite

"Hold on," he said. "How do you eat a sandwich?"

"It's a Buddhist method."

"How is it Buddhist?"

"The sandwich has no beginning or end. It just is."

He reached over and pinched her calf. He had never met anyone like her.

"You're just making stuff up now," he said. "You're saying anything that pops into your mind."

"Anyway," she continued, "the friend of a friend of a friend said you two had hooked up or were dating or something, but then something broke it apart. Maybe me. She thought I could be the cause of that."

"No."

"You don't think I could break up a loving home and family?"

"We kissed once. That's it. Even that was a mistake. It was a bad idea. We both knew it."

"The rumor is that she didn't know it."

"You have a lot of rumors for someone who just came to school a few weeks ago."

"Girl power. We look out for each other."

"I'm not exactly sure what question I'm answering any longer. But for what it's worth, I'm happy where I am. I'm happy being here with you."

"Good. You should be. You kind of need me."

"I do?"

"Of course you do, Zeb. Who else would bring you turkey sandwiches?"

"You have a point."

A dog's snout came up under the cargo door and pushed the gap wider. The black Lab Zeb had seen a few minutes before suddenly tried to climb in with them. Zeb sat up quickly and tried to fend off the dog, but the dog had seen the food and made a slobbering beeline for it. It was kind of funny and kind of terrible.

The dog had an enormous chest and strong legs and for a moment he resembled a guy sticking his head into a huddle of people and asking for a bite to eat. It made Zeb laugh.

"You . . . do . . . not . . . get . . . this . . . foood," Ferron said, pushing the dog off with her legs. "Get out of here!"

"Sorry, sorry, sorry." The dog-walking man appeared and snapped the chain on his dog's collar. "Knock it off, Edgar."

"Edgar?" Ferron asked, her legs still up to protect against a lunge from the dog. "He's a strong boy."

Zeb realized the dog walker was Mr. Kaalkins, the ninth-grade guidance counselor.

"Zeb, that's you!" Mr. Kaalkins said. "And who is this with you?"

"Ferron Ellis. Ferron, this is Mr. Kaalkins."

Mr. Kaalkins held out his hand.

"Nice to meet you, Ferron. You're at Rumney? I don't recognize your name and I know most of the class . . ."

"I came back to town not long ago. Probably about three weeks now."

"Well, a belated welcome. And this is Edgar . . . down, down, down, boy. He's a galoot. Sorry about the dive into the picnic. He might have thought he was climbing into my partner's car. He has a Volvo too."

"It's okay. Is he hungry?"

"He's always hungry, but he doesn't need to eat anything right now. Do you, Edgar? It's almost his dinnertime. Okay, you two, have fun. Zeb . . . gosh, I nearly forgot. Good luck in the big game. I can't make it, unfortunately, but I wish you genuine luck."

"Thank you, Mr. Kaalkins."

"And Ferron, if you need any help settling into the school, my office is right by the main office. I'm almost planted there. No one ever comes to visit, so I would take it as a personal favor if you made it your business to swing by."

"Thank you. I will."

"Mr. Kaalkins, do you think maybe I could stop by sometime to talk about colleges?" Zeb asked. "I'm not really sure what I'm doing next year."

"Sure, Zeb. That's really more Ms. Friedman's area, but of course. I can get you started, maybe give you a few things to think about."

"Thank you."

"It would be my pleasure. Okay, you two . . . enjoy your picnic. Come on, Edgar," Mr. Kaalkins said, dragging the dog away. "You're such a bad boy. A horrible boy . . ."

Zeb looked at Ferron. She opened her eyes wide and made a funny face. Zeb reached out and lowered the door again. What had just happened, he reflected, was a memory.

That day the lab stuck his head in the car. That day. Our first day.

He held her close, his coat a blanket over their shoulders. Rain and sleet continued to dig at the roof. It was nice hearing the rain and knowing it couldn't get to you.

"Are you sleepy?" she whispered.

He shook his head.

"I could be here with you . . ."

"A long time," he finished for her.

She nodded. His hand held hers. They hadn't stopped touching since they'd finished the sandwiches. Zeb had no idea how late it might be. He didn't care, exactly, except for a vague sense that his mother wanted to squeeze in some time with him before the game the next day. He had kissed Ferron a thousand times. She had kissed him too. It had gone back and forth, back and forth, and sometimes it felt like sex and sometimes it felt like love and mostly it felt like both.

"Are you scared about tomorrow? About the game?" she whispered.

It felt wrong, he knew, to raise their voices. They both spoke in whispers.

"Not scared, no."

"What then?"

"Nervous, I guess. Worried that I will let someone down. My teammates, the coaches."

"So if you mess up, it's a bigger deal than if some other guy messes up? Because you're the quarterback?"

He nodded. He didn't want to say something like that. He didn't want it to pass his lips. She twisted up slowly and kissed him.

"I'd be terrified to be out in front of so many people judging me."

"It kind of comes with the territory."

"Still."

"They're nice to you when you do okay, though."

"I don't like crowds as a rule."

"Neither do I. I just like football. I don't really want to, but I should get going," he whispered.

"Me too."

"It was a good sandwich," Zeb said.

"It was a great sandwich."

"I want to see you again."

"When?"

"I don't know. I have the game tomorrow. I don't know when all that will conclude."

"Did you say *conclude*?"

He shrugged.

He kissed her ear and kissed down along her throat. But now things had changed. They had said they were leaving. It was as if, Zeb thought, a magic spell had been broken. As soon as they declared their need to go, the magic began spilling away. Even the interior of the car felt colder.

"I don't know when it will be over tomorrow, but I'd like to see you at some point," he said. "I guess some of it depends on how the game goes."

"Okay."

"But I want to see you."

"I know you do. You're not a fool, after all."

That gave him enough energy to sit up and push the cargo door completely open. The grass leading down to the lake shone pure white. The lake itself had taken on a lacy sheen of ice. He slid out and held out his hands to her. She groaned and inched out.

"This has been one of my favorite days so far," she said, bending back in to stack the sandwich plates inside the wicker hamper. "Top seventeen, probably."

"Just seventeen, huh?"

"Top twenty, at least. You should be grateful."

He limped around and opened her door for her. She climbed inside. She looked at him from her spot behind the wheel.

"That's a first," she said.

"A first what?"

"A boy opening a door for me like that."

"My pleasure."

He closed the door and walked around the back. She started the car. He stood for a moment and looked out at the lake. He thought of the game. He thought of it coming toward him like a snow squall and he tasted winter on his lips. Then he got in the car.

His mother had cooked a nice dinner. He smelled it when he opened the door: garlic bread, his favorite, and meatballs in marinara. He stopped and took a deep breath. He wasn't particularly hungry after the sandwich with Ferron, but he told himself that it was time to do whatever his mother asked. She wasn't able to cook Thanksgiving dinner and she couldn't come to the game, so now was her moment, and he squared his shoulders a little in preparation.

"Zeb? Is that you, honey?"

"It's me, Mom."

"Hope you're good and hungry. I'm cooking your favorite, spaghetti and meatballs. How does that sound? Does that sound good?"

He felt a moment of tenderness seeing her in front of the tiny stove. She had obviously taken some time to clean up the place, and the dinner smelled delicious. She wore a pair of jeans and her favorite at-home sweater, a gray-brown cardigan that zipped up almost to her chin. She had on a pair of tan suede slippers lined with sheep wool, and her hair was still dark from her shower. She smiled when he came closer.

"Smells great," he said, shucking off his coat. "Smells really good, Mom."

"I thought it would be nice . . . you know, just a quiet moment with us. It feels like we're always coming and going and missing each other . . . here, taste the sauce."

She held out a wooden spoon with sauce pooled in the center. She kept her hand under his chin when he tasted it. It tasted terrific. He smiled and nodded. She turned back to the stove. It felt good. It all felt good.

"It's amazing," he said. "Delicious."

"How was practice? Everything all set?"

"Everything is all set."

"I'm hearing about it everywhere!" she said, lifting a glass of wine to her lips and leaning against the counter. "Honestly, I knew it was a big deal . . . of course I knew that, but I had no idea how big a deal this game is. Not really. Lorelei feels horrible about making me come in tomorrow. She really does. She called everyone she knows to cover for me, but it's just not in the cards. You know, I think Arthur is going to go to the game. He said the family needs some representation, and I know he's not family, but he means it in the nicest way, Zeb."

"That's fine. That's nice of Arthur."

"It really is. It is nice of him, isn't it? It really is. He means well, Zeb. I hope you know that."

Zeb nodded. He knew that. He had no problem with Arthur. Arthur had always been decent. Zeb grabbed an iced tea out of the fridge and twisted it open. His mom held up her glass for a toast.

"Here's wishing you the best luck, baby. I'm so proud of you."

"Thanks, Mom."

"So proud. And you look so big and handsome and grown up . . ."

She teared up, her face becoming blurry with pain and happiness and worry. He put his drink aside and hugged her. She cried a little on his shoulder. He had no idea how he could say anything that mattered in that moment. When he let her go, she took a paper towel from a tube on the counter and wiped her eyes carefully, flicking the tears out and away to keep her makeup from smearing.

"I should tell you," she said, turning and washing her hands quickly, "that I invited Uncle Pushee for dinner. I just thought it was important to do that, given the circumstances. He turned me down, but he was nice about it, I'll admit. It's just old business between us."

"It's okay, Mom."

"Maybe it's better with just us two anyway. You know what I thought we could do? I thought maybe you could take me through what will happen tomorrow. You know, give me the real inside scoop. Take me behind the scenes. That way I'll know where you are throughout the morning. A step-by-step kind of thing. How does that sound?"

It didn't sound that great, but Zeb did his best anyway. She stirred the sauce and drank her wine and eventually they ate on the dinette set near the front window of the camper. They hardly ever ate there and they had to move some things—old magazines and catalogs and a bundle of bills—to make space, but Zeb continued telling her whatever he could because he knew she needed to hear it. He answered whatever he could when she asked, and he experienced the strange sensation of seeing his mother as a person apart from himself, as a woman who made spaghetti in a camper and who collected porcelain figurines and dated a man named Arthur who floated outside of her gravitational pull and came into view only when the elements lined up to bring him closer. He saw her as the woman who went over to Uncle Pushee's and invited him to a spaghetti dinner not because she wanted him to be there but because she believed it was something her son might want, and that made him answer her questions more fully, made him more generous in his recounting of anything that might interest her. She took it all in; he watched her pleasure in the knowledge bloom and grow in her face and he realized he had been stingy before, horrible before, to withhold this small gift that was so easy for him to indulge.

"That's all just so wonderful," she said when he finished most of it. "I'm just so blown away by it all. I never expected anything like this to happen."

"Well, it wouldn't have happened if T.T. hadn't been injured."

"Things happen for a reason, Zeb. You never know. Some people have trouble believing that, but I believe it. Tomorrow is going to be a triumph for you. I swear it's in the stars right now. Can't you feel things changing for the better?"

"Maybe so, Mom."

Then she stopped before she said anything else. She cocked her head and at the same time he heard it too. He heard car horns blasting from a long way away. That was strange. You didn't hear cars horns on Redtree Road, but in another ten count he couldn't deny the sound. She looked at him and he saw her face grow to understanding, maybe as his did, and she reached across and put her hand on his.

"Someone said they do this . . ." she said, rising, her face absolutely victorious. "Someone told me this might happen."

"Mom," he said, because he wasn't sure.

Then the horns grew louder. They honked and honked and honked. He put his face in his hands. He knew what it was now. The cheerleaders and well-wishers toilet-papered the houses of the starting players before any important big game. He had only heard about it before. He had never started a game, so no one had ever bothered him, but now he was on a list and the horns kept coming and coming closer.

"Come on, Zeb, come on," his mom said, grabbing him by the elbow. "They're coming to honor you!"

He didn't know if he could do it. He stood carefully, afraid to look at her, afraid his face might show too much. How could he deny her this? How could he speak his embarrassment about the camper and about their circumstances and the dead cars outside Uncle Pushee's house? He stood and let her lead him by the elbow. She hurried him outside and the horns grew greater, louder and louder until they were the only sound, and then they were there, ten, a dozen cars, all the vehicles tagged with streamers and water-soluble paint.

Go Raiders!

Beat Merrymeeting! State champs! Dunham, Otzman, Freckles, Jiler . . . and his name, *Hollowy,* misspelled but written on the back bumper of a maroon Subaru Outback in white crooked letters! Mostly girls. Mostly a pile of girls screaming and laughing and jumping out to heave toilet paper at the camper. Zeb realized someone must have told them where he lived, how he lived, because they did not hesitate. They went right for the camper as if not noticing that it wasn't a house. His mother put her arm through his and when he looked down, he saw such joy in her eyes and face that it pierced him. Just this small thing. Just this one thing in her life and he felt his bottom lip trembling. She squeezed his arm against her side and she waved like a crazy person, laughing uproariously at everything, trying to identify the girls—some wore jerseys and some wore cheerleading sweaters and some simply wore old flannels—and turned constantly to make sure he witnessed what she witnessed.

They did a cheer. He had heard it plenty of times before but had never understood it could be directed to him, could be for him, and that made it different. They jumped and yelled. Someone had a bullhorn that squawked. Some of them, he guessed, had probably been drinking.

Then Zeb saw Stella.

She didn't participate in the cheer. In the crazy headlights, he saw her standing to one side, beautiful, his old friend, and he felt he should go over and say something. It had all been a horrible misunderstanding and he had handled it atrociously, he knew that now, but some things happened that you couldn't take back. He was learning that now. He knew that now.

A girl, C.C. Weller, dodged out of the pack and handed his mom a rose. His mom hugged her, laughing and smiling and turning to look up at him again, and then it was over. Zeb mouthed the word *Sorry* to Stella but wasn't sure she saw it. C.C. held out her hand and knuckle-bumped him. He knuckled-bumped her in return. Then the cars began jockeying backward, pulling out of

Uncle Pushee's drive, their horns again sounding like geese lifting out of a pond on heavy wings while calling to the rest of the V to follow.

Once he had the toilet paper pulled free of the camper, Zeb used a snow shovel to scoop it all into a rubber bin. Uncle Pushee had a small fire going in the outside pit, the Adirondack horseshoe ring that had been a fixture in the yard as long as Zeb could remember.

Uncle Pushee drank a PBR whenever he didn't poke at the fire. Zeb carried the barrelfuls to the fire and dumped them as best he could on the flames. Uncle Pushee herded the wayward pieces deeper into the heart of the fire, the flames rushing in to gobble up the slim paper bundles. Uncle Pushee had used the pretense of a fire to burn off some of his trash. For Uncle Pushee's friends, lighting a fire, Zeb knew, was like turning on a porch light for moths. Whoopie might show up; any of a couple dozen homebrew buddies could arrive just by the scent of smoke in the air.

"Damn foolish business," Uncle Pushee said after the third barrelful. "People could get shot if they go up the wrong driveway. Hell, I was half out of my chair listening when I realized what was coming down my drive."

"Sorry about that. It's a tradition."

Uncle Pushee spat to one side and lifted the PBR can to his lips. He sucked it dry and then crumpled it in one deft motion. He tossed the can on top of the flames. Uncle Pushee didn't recycle and didn't go to the transfer station even on a bet, Zeb knew. He drew another beer out of his coat pocket and leaned his poker in the crook of his arm while he snapped open the PBR. Then he nudged a box of frozen peas and a milk carton into the fire. Both caught without much negotiating.

Zeb tried not to think about his knee. It hurt quite a bit. He felt somewhat guilty for not resting it more, but the day had been a good one anyway. More than good, honestly. Even now, bringing paper trash to Uncle Pushee, felt proper. He limped on his last two loads. If Uncle Pushee noted it, he didn't say anything.

"They do this to all the players?" Uncle Pushee asked, seemingly bemused by the notion of people dumping trash on one another's homes. "Hell of a mess to deliver to hard-working families."

"Just before the big games," Zeb said, putting the snow shovel down and leaning on it. "State championship games . . ."

"I don't know where you got this sports fixation. Not from me, that's for sure. Nobody around here encouraged it. It's all your onions, believe me."

"It's just fun. I like playing. I always have."

"Your dad was some quick on his feet, let me tell you. Ran like a deer. He could turn off the light and be under the covers before it was dark."

Zeb had heard that a million times, but it still pleased him to hear it.

"I'm not so fast. I have a good arm, though."

"Do you, now? Y'can huck it out there, huh?"

"Not bad."

"Fellow who comes in for tires yesterday . . . wants a pair of Pirellis and I tell him they ain't worth a dog's snot in the snow, but he says that's all he wants. Anyway, he says the betting line is on Merrymeeting. Is that how you see it?"

"Probably be close."

"This is a pretty shrewd fellow, let me tell you. He says you're a seven-point, maybe eight-point underdog."

"I suppose."

"I guess we won't know until we know."

"That's the way it usually goes."

Uncle Pushee pushed some more papers into the fire. He had paper bags filled with bills and envelopes and paper plates. The flames grabbed hold of the paper and turned yellow.

Zeb's phone dinged with an incoming message and he looked at it to see a note from Stella.

WTF????? Was that yr house?

He deleted the message as fast as he could and buried his phone back in his pocket. He felt his skin turn red. He had trouble breathing for a moment.

"Your mom to bed?" Uncle Pushee asked.

"I think so."

"She invited me for dinner."

"I know."

"Better to keep things the way they are. Good fences make good neighbors."

"I guess."

"Whoopie said he might be by. He's going to bring some burn-off."

"I think I should hit it."

"How's your knee feel?"

Zeb shrugged.

"Nothing I hate more than a bum knee," Uncle Pushee said, drinking hard on his PBR. "Can't dance so much as a jig with a bum knee."

"It's got to be okay tomorrow."

"Oh, it will be right as rain. You'll see. The body knows things like that. It knows when it needs to behave."

"Hope so."

"Prop it up on some pillows tonight and you'll be solid as a post tomorrow."

"Okay, then. Good night, Uncle Pushee."

"Good luck tomorrow, Zeb. I'll be pulling for you."

"It should be on the radio."

"Might just have to tune it in," Uncle Pushee said, fishing out more papers and pushing them into the flames with the poker. He looked like a man feeding a cannon. "You'll do fine. You got the grit."

"Thanks, Uncle Pushee."

"Right as rain tomorrow. You wait and see. Right as rain."

He had trouble sleeping. Not so much falling asleep, but staying asleep. He had the feeling again that things needed to move somehow. Part of the feeling came from Uncle Pushee outside burning off paper with Whoopie and a few other fellows who had come by. He heard the beer cans crushing when each man finished his drink, then the pause, then the tinny toss as the can landed on the rocks surrounding the fire. Later he heard a big uproar and someone yelling in a woody voice that clanged and broke through the quiet night. He listened to the men and thought about Stella, about the girls throwing toilet paper at the camper, and what people might say in the backs of their throats about how he lived. He thought about his mom, too, and how she had eaten things up with a spoon, an enormous spoon, so happy to have the weight of everyday life lifted off her shoulders for a moment. All those thoughts, all those currents, stirred him up.

He took up his phone and texted Ferron. He had texted her earlier but she hadn't answered. Now he asked her if she had broken up with him, wrote *Ha-ha* after it, then deleted the whole thing. Instead he wrote: *You there?*

Sleepy.

Too sleepy?

We watched a movie.

Just saying good night.

Good night, Zeb. I like writing your name.

He smiled when he got that. He put the phone to his forehead and tried to think.

Can't fall asleep.

Understandable. Try counting Ferrons.

I've only counted one.

One is all any man needs.

R Ferrons so rare?

Yes.

What movie did u watch?

Trainwreck. Pretty good. U c it?

No.

I liked today.

Me too.

A lot.

Me too.

Can we get together after the game?

Probably. Yes. I hope so.

My dad watched the public access call-in show about the game tomorrow.

What did he think?

Not much. He said it was interesting. Did you watch?

No, I didn't want to hear them talking about T.T.

I don't blame you.

What did they say?

I didn't pay much attention. Dad said they talked about you. Said you had a good arm.

That's something.

Coach K ooked old, Dad said.

Ooked old?

Looked old. Sorry. Sleepy. Good night, Zeb. Sending you good dreams.

I need good dreams.

We can dream of each other. Let's learn to do that.

Yes.

Where do you think we go when we sleep?

Alabama.

I always thought so. Good night.

Good night.

Wind hit the side of the camper later and brought him awake. He heard Mr. Television crying and went to the back door to let the stupid creature inside. Mr. Television didn't want to enter once the door finally opened, so Zeb bent down and picked him up. He closed the back door with his hip, slipped the bungee that held it fastened over the towel rack, and carried Mr. Television back to the couch with him. He stretched out under the covers and put Mr. Television on his chest. He made a quiet crowd noise sound in his throat and made Mr. Television pretend to take a snap from center. He held Mr. Television's tiny paws as if he were a QB, then made Mr. Television back up and pretend to throw the ball. The ball went through the air and Zeb stuck Mr. Television's arms straight up, signaling a touchdown, and Zeb made the crowd go wild, made Mr. Television dance a little in acceptance, then the wind hit the side of the camper again and he saw sparks fling themselves past the back window. Uncle Pushee might still be awake, might still be sitting beside the fire, for all Zeb knew, though he had gone silent. Zeb listened for a while to detect any sounds, but nothing came. When the next wind blew, Mr. Television jumped down from the couch and went to the back door. He cried until Zeb stood and let him out. By then, to his surprise, Zeb could see the faint outline the morning had dusted onto the world.

SATURDAY 8

Coach K regarded them all carefully. Zeb watched him. He realized he had been observing this man for three years and he still didn't know what made the coach tick. One way or the other, the man had their interest as he stood at the front of the cafeteria, the knife-and-fork sounds fading as if he had commanded it. Someone pulled out a chair a little and it squeaked on the tile floor. Though Coach K did not turn to identify the maker of the sound, it clearly offended him. Nothing in this particular universe could move without his permission.

"We are going to the University of New Hampshire football field in Durham. The ride should take a little under two hours. For the next twenty minutes or so, fans and parents and well-wishers are going to want to pat you on the back and wish you good luck. Nothing wrong with that. Nothing wrong with any of it. It's as it should be."

Coach K rowed his eyes slowly over the cafeteria. Zeb did not try to meet the coach's eyes, nor did he refuse their contact. Hawny sat beside him. Hawny, he knew, would be aping this speech about ten minutes after it concluded. Still, you couldn't pretend it wasn't a solemn moment. Coach K put his right foot up on the seat of a chair in front of him and leaned forward.

"I am here to tell you that I guarantee you will win. I don't mean the score. No one can predict that, although there have been plenty of opinions this week about the outcome of this game. Opinions are just that, opinions, and they're usually poorly informed. Trust me about that."

He leaned farther toward the table. Zeb felt his teammates leaning forward, hanging on what their coach had to say, and Coach K nodded as if he understood his power over them.

"So you ask yourself, *How can he guarantee a win and then say in the same breath that no one can predict the outcome?* Right? You've been thinking that. Here's what I want to say. You can win if you play the game the way you love the game. It's as simple as that, boys. Play it like you love it. When you were little boys and you went out in the backyard and played with your friends, you won. You won when you came to practice that first day back in August . . ."

Some players groaned and everyone laughed.

". . . and you've won every day since. Every day you've come to practice, you've won. Now let it loose. It's not just about effort, although effort counts. It's about the joy of the game, boys. Play it joyfully, play it full out, and you will win no matter the outcome. Do you understand me? Those well-wishers and those pundits who claim to know what can and can't happen in a game . . . they are not in your heart. Look around you. These other players . . . your teammates . . . you play for them and you play for your own joy, and if you do that, win, lose, or draw, you're going to be victorious today. That's the promise I make you."

He slid his foot off the chair and nodded at Coach Hoch. Coach Hoch hopped up and told them to finish breakfast. He said the buses would be leaving in fifteen. Behind him, Coach K lifted a coffee cup and held it toward Dino. Zeb watched Dino scuttle off for the coffeepot. Coach K sat down next to Coach Larantino and presumably resumed a conversation he had been having with him.

"I look at you and I feel such joy," Hawny said, starting in and mopping up his eggs with the corner of his toast. "I feel my boner rise."

"Shut up, Hawny."

"Nice people don't say shut up."

"We should get going," Zeb said, pushing his plate away. He couldn't eat much. His stomach felt jittery. Before Hawny could answer, Mrs. Gilmore came by. She wore her trainer jacket and new white sneakers. Someone had painted *Go Raiders* on her cheek in blue and white. Her breath smelled of coffee when she leaned close.

"How's it feeling today, Zeb?" she asked.

"Not bad."

"You come right up to the training room when we get to Durham, okay? We're getting the trainer for the UNH team to tape you. That should give you a little more support. You'll be able to trust it. I've seen him work. He does a great job. Tops in his field."

"Yes, ma'am."

"How about me?" Hawny asked.

"We'll tape your head, Hawny. How would that be?"

"Oh, Mrs. Gilmore, you have hurt my feelings."

Zeb felt Mrs. Gilmore pat his shoulder. She moved down the row of chairs, stopping to ask about this or that player. A few players had already returned their plates to the cafeteria tray window. Zeb was about to get up when Dino suddenly appeared at his shoulder. Dino looked frazzled and busy. He was in charge of the equipment and that was no joke today.

"Coach K wants to see you for a minute," Dino said. "Before you get on the bus."

"Now?"

"Sure, now works. He wants to check on your knee."

Zeb pushed onto his feet and slid his tray to Hawny. Hawny nodded. Zeb touched knuckles with half a dozen players as he made his way to the faculty table. Everyone seemed jazzed, Zeb reflected. He wondered if you could tell how a team would do just by looking at it. From his experience, he knew a pumped-up team sometimes fell flat and vice versa. He pegged the Rumney Raiders at about an eight on a scale of one to ten. He had no idea if that was a good place to be or not.

"Have a seat, Zeb," Coach K said when Zeb reached him. Coach K pushed out a wooden chair with his foot and lifted his coffee cup at the same time. "How's the knee?"

"Feels great."

"You sure, son? I'm the one person you need to level with. All these guys around here . . . you tell them that the knee is great. But I need to know the truth so I can help us win."

"It feels great, honestly."

Coach K smiled. Most of the table had cleared now. The coaches had filed out to begin herding the kids onto the bus. Zeb knew he was more or less alone with Coach K, something that had rarely happened before.

"I admire you," Coach K said. "When I was your age . . . with a big game to play . . . heck, I would've said my knee was fine too. Okay, we'll go with your diagnosis. But promise me, if you feel you can't legitimately play at some point during the game, you tell me. This isn't the time for heroics. You at half speed with a bum knee will not help us, you understand me? We want our best chance to win."

"Yes, sir."

"You're an interesting kid, Zeb. You stayed on the team even when it was clear you happened to be behind one of the best players in our state's history. You stuck it out. Coach Steve pointed that out to me. I guess I hadn't really stopped to think about it from your perspective."

Zeb nodded. He didn't think he had anything to add to that.

"That took guts. That shows grit. You taught me to look a little harder at the second-teamers. Sometimes we focus only on the players who are easy to spot. I'll try to be better about that in the future."

"Yes, sir."

"Do you have any questions? Anything troubling you?"

"No, sir."

"It's just a game, Zeb. Don't let it get too big in your head. You can handle it. A lot of people will be watching, but for them it's just something to do on a Saturday. You are a player. You're playing in a state championship game. That's something to enjoy and feel proud about."

"I do, sir."

"Okay, get on the bus. Good luck today, Zeb. You're going to do fine."

"Yes, sir."

Coach K held out his hand. Zeb shook it. Then he went to get on the bus.

The well-wishers stood in a pool around the team bus. Zeb recognized many of them. Moms and dads, boosters, former players. The cheerleaders stood at the entrance to the bus, all of them dressed in their outfits. They wore blue ribbons in their hair and every one of the girls had *Go Raiders* scripted on her cheeks. They fluttered their pompoms as the team started boarding, and Zeb saw Stella. He wished he had another way to enter the bus, but this was it, they were being funneled forward, and he could not escape going directly past her.

"Sorry," he whispered when he stood beside her, waiting for the players in front of him to board, "I am. I am really sorry."

"Tell someone who cares," she said, shaking her pompom at Dunham.

"It was my fault. All mine—"

"Fuck off, Zeb."

That was it. He boarded the bus. The team mascot, Ronny the Raider, sat in the back seat. He wore a pirate's outfit, complete with a cardboard cutlass. The kid's real name was Jeffy Williams. He was a tenth-grader, Zeb knew, a kid with Down syndrome. He lived and died to be the Raider. He loved wearing the costume.

A few car horns honked as Zeb swung into a seat midway back in the bus. Hawny sat with him. Hawny had a copy of the *North Country News*. The front cover read: RAIDERS TRAVEL TO DURHAM

FOR STATE CHAMPIONSHIP. Underneath the banner headline the editors had run a team picture beside a profile shot of Coach K leaning over McCay and Jiler on the blocking sled. The photo was from the beginning of the season during double sessions in early September. At the bottom of the paper, an ad from Tedeski's Quik Mart said: RAIDERS RULE! GOOD LUCK, TEAM! The store offered seventy-five cents off a midday Monster Meal with the coupon attached to the ad.

"Where did you get that?" Zeb asked Hawny.

"The boosters handed them out. Man, did you see Mr. McCloskey? He was all raging wild already. He's got to be hitting the sauce, I tell you. Bloody marys for Mr. Mc."

"Do you ever think it's weird how everyone makes such a big deal of the game?"

"It is a big deal."

"Why, though? It's just a game."

Hawny fluffed the newspaper to read it better.

"It says here Merrymeeting has the best defense in the state. It says it's smothering. It also says you suck."

"It does not."

"No, it says stuff like, the Raiders will miss their star quarterback, T.T. Monroe. It just infers that you suck."

"Infers? That's a good word, Hawny."

"Isn't it? My vocabulary is expanding. I think I'm getting smarter."

"You can't help but go up."

Hawny leaned across Zeb and looked out at the cheerleaders. When he leaned back, he shook his head.

"You're telling me that you and Stella . . ."

"Drop it, would you? I don't want to think about all that."

"I mean, she was into you?"

"Just drop it, Hawny."

Hawny wouldn't drop it, Zeb knew, but the ignition rattled on and that saved him. The engine backfired and that brought a roar from the people crowding around the bus entrance. Good omen or bad omen, Zeb couldn't say, but his stomach ratcheted up a notch with nerves. This was it. He held out his hand and knuckle-bumped Hawny. Hawny knuckle-bumped him and folded down the paper. The rule was to be quiet on the bus. No talking, no cell phones, no papers, no books, nothing.

The bus wobbled from a stationary spot and began chugging out of the parking lot. Zeb turned around and saw three buses followed theirs. The cheerleaders climbed on the second bus when it paused to pick them up. They ran up the stairs and then the procession gathered speed. A bunch of private cars fell in line and began honking their horns. Kids hung out the windows of the cars and screamed and yelled and blew air horns up into the sky. Zeb put his head forward against the seat in front of him and tried to calm himself.

When they arrived at UNH, Zeb went straight to the training room. Dr. Deke, an enormous black man with a full beard, gray in patches, ran the UNH training room. Zeb almost knocked before he stepped inside. He wore his girdle pads, a loose Raiders T-shirt, and a pair of blue flip-flops. The entire walk to the training room he had tried to determine how his knee felt. How it really felt. He knew it wasn't 100 percent, but he also knew it had improved since the initial injury. Call it 80 percent, he told himself. Maybe a little more.

Dr. Deke wore a white cotton beanie. The hat looked good on him. Soft jazz played in the background of the room. A girl trainer pushed a broom around the taping tables, her hair tucked into the hatband of a Patriots ball cap. Dr. Deke had evidently been razzing her, because the girl played at taking extra attention with her sweeping. A window overlooking the field let in a cool stream of air.

"You Zeb?" Dr. Deke asked. "You must be, right? Knee tape?"

"Yes, sir."

"You've come to the right place. Dr. Deke's magic-potion show."

"Some magic," said the girl.

"You see the conditions under which I work?" Dr. Deke asked, his large hand patting the padded taping table in the center of the room. "No respect."

"My trainer, Mrs. Gilmore, said I should report here."

"You're the QB, man! You're the king today. Hop on up here. We'll get you straightened out."

For Zeb and the rest of the team, it was a big day, but to Dr. Deke and his young assistant, it was simply another day. Zeb walked to the table and climbed up on it. He had never had anything taped for a game. In fact, before Mrs. Gilmore had taped him for the last few practices, he had never been taped at all. He wasn't sure it did much good when you got right down to it. He had read online that the taping most athletes received was largely psychological. Tape, all tape, loosened in about ten minutes under game conditions, according to the article.

Mrs. Gilmore appeared at Zeb's shoulder. She still wore *Go Raiders* scripted on her cheek.

"How you feeling, Zeb?" Mrs. Gilmore asked. "The knee okay?"

"Yes, ma'am."

"We're doing a lateral?" Dr. Deke asked Mrs. Gilmore.

Mrs. Gilmore nodded.

"We'll give you some support for your side-to-side motion, Zeb," she said. "That's the best we can do. I think you'll be okay. Dr. Deke can fix you up if anyone can. If you weren't playing a game, we'd just tell you to stay off it and let it mend on its own. But Dr. Deke can do magic, I promise."

Dr. Deke nodded and began taping. He worked fast and tight. Clearly he had taped a thousand knees, because his hands never slowed or faltered. The tape went on flat and smooth and even. In no time he had finished and he told Zeb to climb down and try it out. Zeb slid onto his feet and bounced a little at Dr. Deke's suggestion. Mrs. Gilmore bent down and ran her hand over his knee.

"How much flex do you have?" she asked.

Zeb demonstrated what he could do with his leg. He flexed it back like a horse waiting to be shod. Mrs. Gilmore nodded.

"Be natural on it, but play within yourself, if you know what I mean. Try to stay away from really big movements on it. Do you know how to do that?"

"Yes, ma'am."

"You'll be okay, son," Dr. Deke said. "You've got a Dr. Deke guarantee."

A half dozen players arrived from the other side of the training room. Merrymeeting players, Zeb slowly realized. It shocked him somehow to see them as fellow players seeking medical treatment. An older man with a white beard accompanied them. Maybe he was a trainer, like Mrs. Gilmore, or maybe he was an assistant coach. Either way, he held the players back with an outstretched arm. It all made sense when you broke it down, Zeb realized, but he hadn't been prepared to see his opponents as humans.

"Send any of the other players up in a few minutes," Mrs. Gilmore said. "Tell Otzman we'll get him next. Bring Billy too. We're closing in on time. Am I forgetting anyone?"

"No, ma'am, I don't think so."

"Good luck today, Zeb," Dr. Deke said and held out his hand for a knuckle-bump. "Do your best."

"Yes, sir. Thank you, sir."

Zeb left the training room, sensing the tightness that now wrapped around his leg. It felt good. It felt better. It felt like he could play on it.

Zeb had just made it back to the locker room when T.T. Monroe walked in on crutches. Zeb didn't see him at first. Instead, he had a general sense that something had changed the air. Then a few players rose and someone shouted and then people began clapping. Zeb turned his head to see what had started things and he saw T.T. T.T. wore his Raiders jersey and a blue Dallas Cowboys hat. His leg carried a long, heavy bandage, but T.T. seemed easy on the crutches, able to move and swing himself around with typical ease and grace.

"Lord love a duck, look who just walked in the locker room,"

Hawny said, leaning back on the bench to get a better look. "No word for the whole week, then he shows up on game day. The great and powerful Oz."

"He is still part of the team, Hawny. Give him a break."

"Is he? Seems like showboating to me."

"You're too hard on him. The guy probably had a pretty rough week."

"He's an ass."

Zeb didn't love to admit it to himself, but he didn't much like T.T. being there either. But T.T. was still his teammate, a great one at that, and Zeb stood and walked over to where T.T. shook hands with the other players. Zeb had a strange sense that they had something to share as quarterbacks, as leaders, but he couldn't say what it was. Perhaps the team needed to see a unified front. Truth was, they had run a million drills together, jogged laps together, played catch together. That counted for something, Zeb figured. Like it or not, football bound them side by side. Zeb decided to keep it light and easy. When the other players cleared, he held out his hand and felt T.T. take it.

"QB!" T.T. said, raising his voice in a singsong chant. "How's it feeling? How you doing, Zeb, man?"

"Not bad. Feeling good."

"You always had that arm, man. Smooth arm. Slow as a camel, but you could throw!"

"Not going to win it running, that's for sure."

"No, I guess not. I guess that's not the game plan today."

Then they exchanged a look. Zeb wondered even as the look passed between them what it might signify. Man-to-man bull-crap.

Stella bull-crap. Quarterback mutual regard. Fortunately, Coach Hoch came in and grabbed T.T. in a bear hug. T.T. had to hop on one leg to remain upright. He nearly lost one of his crutches.

"How's it going, T.T.?" Coach Hoch asked, pushing him back to look at him. "They did the procedure . . . that came out okay? I'm surprised they let you travel."

"Fine and dandy, Coach. They get you right up on your feet after surgery. They don't baby you, I'll tell you that much. Besides, I wanted to get back to see the game."

"Good, good, good. Glad to hear that. So glad. We'll miss you today, T.T., but we've got a good man here. Solid man. Zeb has accepted the mantle."

"All the way," T.T. said. "All the way."

Zeb knuckle-bumped quickly with T.T. and headed back to finish dressing. Hawny had his shoulder pads on and his jersey half pulled down. He turned around and Zeb finished jerking down the jersey. Hawny nodded and went back to dressing. Zeb glanced at the huge digital clock that hung between the two doors to the shower. A sign above the clock read IS IT YOUR TIME? The clock counted down until it was time to take the field. Seventeen minutes and thirty-five seconds. Zeb flexed his knee when he slid it into his padded pants. The tape caught for a moment before releasing his leg to stab more deeply into the leg hole. He slid in the other leg and then stood to adjust his belt. When he glanced back at the clock, only the seconds had ticked away. He still had seventeen minutes to be whatever he was before he became the thing he hoped to be.

• • •

The TV feed suddenly came on in the locker room. It played from an enormous monitor hung from a bare space beneath the upstairs training rooms. It popped off a second later, then came on more surely, the crowd loud, the commentators speaking with their fingers held to their ears so they could hear properly.

"Shut that thing off," Coach Larantino yelled up to the training room. "We don't want that down here. Turn it off."

Nobody heard him. Or maybe no one knew how to turn it off. The volume went up temporarily until sound flooded the room. Zeb tried not to look, but he couldn't help it. The stands were crowded and the broadcast seemed almost professional and polished. He recognized one of the commentators. He had been calling games for years around the state, but the other guy, the younger one, was less familiar. While they talked, a stream of kids walked behind them, sometimes stopping to yell something at the camera. A few Merrymeeting fans walked by dressed in green. One kid stopped and blew his air horn as loud as he could. The commentators smiled and grimaced at the noise.

"As you can see, the crowd is—"

The TV cut off.

"Prime time!" someone shouted.

"We're on TV, man," Hawny whispered next to him. "Freaking badass, man."

Zeb couldn't sit still. Little shining thoughts snapped into his head and flew right out. He knew his mom would have the television turned to the game at the restaurant. He pictured her stopping on her way to tables, plates in hand, just to watch a play or two. People would probably get annoyed with the service, but that was okay. Even Uncle Pushee might tune his radio to the game.

"We got this, man." Hawny said, turning to Zeb.

"Sure we do."

"I mean it."

"So do I."

"Just play football. Just shoot your deer."

"I will."

"I'm proud of you, man. No matter what happens. I'm proud of you."

"Thanks, Hawny."

The TV came on again, then blinked right off. Zeb caught a glimpse of the Merrymeeting cheerleaders. They had made a pyramid for the camera and the girl on top stood above everyone and lifted her hands in a touchdown signal. A few seconds later, the officials came through the locker room. They had a crew of six. They smiled as they went by.

"Good luck today, boys," the last man in line said.

When they pushed open the door to go out, Zeb heard more air horns and someone playing a drum. The sounds seemed to catch in his guts and rattle around. He put his head down low, by his shins, and breathed for a second. When he sat back up, Hawny asked him if he was going to faint.

"Hell no," Zeb said.

"Good. You know those Merrymeeting kids aren't deer hunters like we are, right?" Hawny said. "They've never been out in the woods like we have."

"Shhh. You don't know that."

"You've got something they don't have."

"Shut up, Hawny. You're driving me nuts."

Zeb closed his eyes and pictured throwing a ball. He pictured it coming out of his hand. He felt the laces leaving his fingertips and sensed the ball moving into its spiral. He could throw. That's what he could depend on.

The temperature display read 39 degrees, and it looked like it might start raining at any minute.

Zeb paused while Dunham, the fullback, began shouting that it was game time. He shouted it two or three times, then broke into a call-and-response:

"What time is it?"

"Game time."

"What time is it?"

"Our time."

That had been their ritual since the start of the season.

Zeb leaned forward, extended his hand, and shouted with the other players.

"One, two, *three!*" Dunham yelled.

"Raiders!"

"Who?"

"Raiders!"

"Who?"

"Raiders!"

The last response disappeared in barks of boys too emotional to contain themselves. Zeb stepped spryly to one side to preserve his knee. The team exploded onto the east end of the stadium, its appearance met with air horns and whistles. Zeb trotted carefully, nursing the knee, doing his best to keep things level. The cheerleaders had formed a gauntlet and he ran down the center, only

Jeffy, the Rumney Raider, keeping his pace. Jeffy stabbed with his cardboard cutlass at anyone who looked at him.

Zeb saw Stella and veered to the opposite side of the parallel lines to avoid her.

"Here you go, here you go, here you go," Coach Steve shouted, his face red and strong, his mouth an open tunnel of tongue and teeth. "Here we go, Raiders . . . line up for cal, line it up . . . here we go, big day, here we go."

Zeb had nearly passed by when Coach Steve grabbed him. Zeb felt the coach squeeze him.

"Your day," Coach Steve whispered. "Your day, Zeb, no one can take it away."

"Yes, sir."

"All your life, you've been pointing toward this day. Your day. Now hop in line for cal, but stretch it out good, okay? Easy does it."

Then Zeb stepped on the actual field inside the sidelines. It was a beautiful field with bright white stripes and a lawn the color of a spring leaf. The numbers marking the various yard stripes shone white and pure. Zeb kept his eyes down. He sent his thoughts to his knee, scanning it, but he felt too excited to discern much. He trotted slowly to his usual position beside Hawny for calisthenics. Hawny stood at the back of the squad, last line. Nutville, he called it. But even Hawny looked psyched today. He pounded his thigh pads, then clapped, pounded again, clapped. It was a war drum and Zeb pulled up next to Hawny and knuckle-bumped. Then he began pounding his own thigh pads, *pound, pound, clap, pound, pound clap, pound, pound clap.* In front of the squad, Dunham pounded like a crazy man. Twice he broke from the rhythm to sprint up and down the line, his hand out to slap five with the seniors in the front, the crowd going nutty each time he did it.

When he came back to the center of the field, he spun quickly and broke down, squaring up, and the entire squad stopped on his count, all eyes riveted on him. Zeb followed. Then Dunham snapped to attention and did a jumping jack and the entire team followed, cracking loud on the "One, two, *three,*" and Zeb felt the beauty of belonging, of having reliable teammates, guys who would fight beside you, stay by you.

They had hit twelve when the Merrymeeting squad poured onto the field.

Merrymeeting did not come on in any kind of order; they flooded onto the field like a dam letting loose a pocket of water. Whatever sounds Rumney had been making suddenly got swept away by the crowd response to the wild jubilant run of the team onto the field. No, not water, Zeb decided, revising his earlier thought; something like a vine moving in fast motion to take over a trellis. Merrymeeting had always had green and white uniforms, but today, in preparation for the state championship, Zeb imagined, they had found uniforms of pure green. Green jerseys, green pants, green helmets. The colors struck Zeb as obscenely flashy but badass too, and he felt the knowledge pass around his own team as they tried not to watch the intensity of the Merrymeeting charge. Despite himself, Zeb found his eyes searching out Manza, the top defensive player on the Merrymeeting squad. You couldn't mistake him, Zeb saw, because Manza stood about six foot seven, weighed nearly three hundred pounds, and was rumored to be all muscle. His green uniform looked insane. He looked like a giant tree swaggering onto the field, and Zeb wondered how such a player could be blocked, who on his team could take on that assignment. Almost as if he understood the question, Manza trotted out to the fifty-yard line and pointed at the Rumney squad, shouting something Zeb couldn't make out, clearly mocking them. Coach K would never have permitted such a display, not ever, but Merrymeeting had a young coach named Furyes who had a story of playing loose with the rules, cutting corners, and that fit the Merrymeeting style.

Manza grabbed his hips and pretended to fuck the Rumney team.

It was a fleeting gesture, but Zeb saw it. So did the other guys on the squad. Hawny in mid–jumping jack started laughing as Manza danced back to join his team.

"Did he just pump at us?" Hawny yelled. "What a jackass! But he's kind of bringing it on. You have to give him that."

"They're green" was all Zeb could think to say.

"They look like broccoli. Ugliest uniforms ever. That's official."

"They look like something. I don't know what they look like."

"They look like pond scum, that's what."

But they didn't. Zeb knew their appearance had made an impact on the Rumney team. He felt it himself. Merrymeeting looked wild and unpredictable. They had already won something and the game hadn't yet begun.

Zeb threw easy at first, clicking on short squares and slants over the center. He wanted to get his feet in position properly, to drop back, set up, then release. It hurt to push off when he threw, but otherwise it felt okay. His arm had a good snap to it. The ball came off his fingers in a tight spiral. It was all right. It was all going to be all right. For the first time since entering the field, he looked around and took a deep breath.

It was not very crowded when you observed it objectively. People ringed around the lowest level; the upper level was empty except for a few kids who looked to be playing some sort of tag game up in the runways. Call it ten thousand, Zeb guessed. True, it was on television, broadcast on NH Public TV Channel 11, but Zeb doubted many people took time out of their Saturdays to watch a high school football game. Still, it was more people than Zeb had ever played in front of, more than he had been able to picture. The Merrymeeting side of the field, the west side, had *greened out.* Every single fan wore green. They wanted to be aggressively green, in your face monochromatic, and Zeb had to hand it to them—it worked. He felt the color getting under his skin.

Zeb threw a down and out and up. He winged it. The ball traveled in a firm arc forty yards downfield. It led Gray, a long, bony tight end, by two steps. The ball landed harmlessly on the ground and bounced straight up. Gray snagged it on the first hop.

Zeb could throw. He felt that. That wouldn't be a problem.

"Let's run a few plays down on the end zone, a few plays, here we go," Coach Hoch yelled, his voice scrambled and nerved up. Zeb trotted the length of half the field and took the team into the huddle. He knelt in the center of the huddle carefully, taking his time, deliberately slowing things so that his team would not be too keyed up. He saw the tension on everyone's face. He wondered if he should try to say something funny to get them to relax, but he wasn't very good at that sort of thing, he knew.

"Let's run a forty-one sweep, on two, ready . . . break."

Easy play. A handoff to Otzman on a sweep left. At the snap Otzman folded over the ball and sprinted around the corner. McCay, the guard, pulled in front of him. It looked good. It looked crisp. They had been running the play since late August.

"Okay, okay, okay," Coach Hoch called. "Get a little samba in the old legs. Loosen up. Today's the day, boys. This is your day."

While the team came back to him, Zeb scanned the Rumney side of the grandstand. For a moment, everyone blurred together, but then, slowly, he began to pick out familiar faces. He spotted some of the boosters sitting higher than the other fans, and, still scanning, he located Arthur. His eye almost ran past him, but when he concentrated he saw Arthur sitting alone on a cushion. He appeared to be reading the game program. Zeb felt tied up seeing Arthur there. He knew Arthur would report back to Zeb's mom. He would probably call at half, or text at least. Arthur's presence made Zeb think of his father. It made him think of not having a father.

Zeb called a straight dive for Dunham.

On the snap, he handed Dunham the ball. Dunham poked through the line and sprinted out of the end zone. He slammed the ball down on his way back. That was a little goofy, Zeb thought. He hadn't scored and he hadn't won anything. Running a dive in pregame wasn't exactly heroic.

After a half dozen more plays it was done. Coach Hoch whistled them back to the locker room. They only had fourteen minutes to kickoff. Because the game was televised, Zeb supposed, pregame felt compressed. They had to move along. Going back to the locker room was a chance to use the men's room once more, then that was that. Whatever would happen was about to happen. That was the truth. It made Zeb feel strange inside to know that.

"Take care of yourself, then huddle up. Let's go, move along. Let's go."

Coach Hoch's voice sounded too loud in the locker room after being outside, and Zeb ignored it as much as he could. He wished he had some sort of ritual to follow. Other players, starters, had an entire season to hone their pregame rituals, but this was his first start and he didn't have an established pattern. Usually he would be joking with Hawny.

Coach K waited in the center of the room for everyone to stop moving. Zeb used the restroom, then took a seat on the bench beside his locker. The clock between the shower doors said seven minutes. Zeb couldn't quiet his mind. Things slammed through in no particular order. He thought of the orange Fanta, and of a deer he had once hunted up on Sally Ridge, and of a stream in the White Mountains that had collected so many autumn leaves into its center that it had shone gold and red—like a metal bar—the water moving over it like glass melting. He thought of Coach Adams, the college coach who had sent him the brochures from Emporia State. He thought of the guidance counselor Mr. Kaalkins and how he would go see him no matter what happened in the game. He thought of Uncle Pushee, and of his mom, and of Arthur sitting out watching the game all alone, and he could not get his mind to stop until Coach K spoke his first words.

"Men, we are going out to play for the New Hampshire state championship in just a few minutes. This is a game, I promise you, that you will remember the rest of your life. Have your moment now. Have it here. Do it for each other. Do it for your families and your communities. We don't need to yell and shout. That's not our way. Let's go out and show them what Rumney Raider football is all about. Let's go out and play as we know we can play. What do you say? Is it time? Are we ready?"

That brought everyone up. Zeb stood and felt his heart slam against his ribs. His arms and legs trembled. Dunham let out the cry of the banshee and then it was over. They moved in a hive for the field. Zeb felt everything buzzing, everything alive, everything different somehow. He tried to stay calm. Then the air horns hit him and he saw the cheerleaders, Stella right there, and the game waited for him, the green of Merrymeeting already shimmering like a tide.

Zeb felt Coach K's hand on his elbow. Zeb tried to control his breathing. Rumney had received the kick and run it back to the thirty-seven-yard line. Now it was offense. Now it was his time. His mind felt blank. It felt as if he couldn't remember a single play. He told himself that was nonsense. He told himself it would be fine if he could calm down and relax. That was a tall order, though. That was a very tall order, because suddenly the stadium seemed louder.

"Here we go, here we go," Coach K said, apparently listening to the earphones that connected him to the spotting booth above. "Okay, they're keeping Manza on the right of the defense . . . your blind side, though. Keep him in mind, Zeb. We may run at him, but let's start a boom right. Let's run Otzman, okay? Let's get a taste of blood and then go from there."

Zeb nodded. He nodded, worried that he had misheard the words even as he tried to listen. He looked at Coach K, wondering if he had finished with his instructions. Evidently he had, because he slapped Zeb on the shoulder pads and stepped back behind the sideline. Coach Hoch, meanwhile, yelled something to the offensive line, then turned around and hissed at the sideline players to step back.

Zeb ran onto the field.

"Here we go, here we go," Dunham yelled. "Bring it, bring it, bring it."

"Okay, we're going right off tackle. Let's block hard. Let's make it crisp."

"Call the fucking play," McCay said.

McCay always talked.

"Don't you fucking talk in my huddle," Zeb said. "Shut your mouth, McCay."

McCay took a step forward, ready to fight, but Jiler stepped between them.

"Would you two wankers shut the fuck up? Call the play!"

Zeb called it. The team broke. Zeb followed them to the line.

And that was when he first felt Manza. Manza was too big. He was obscenely big for a high school player. It was like a bad joke, or a cartoon, to see him lined up with the others, waiting. Notre Dame had already signed him to a full ride. He was already as big as a pro.

"You dancing?" Manza yelled, his hands moving, his fingers twinkling like a safe cracker's fingers loosening before touching the safe's dial. "Who's dancing with me? Come on and dance, honey bun. Yo, Holloway, I'll dance your fucking head off. I'll snap you in half."

Zeb smiled. It was kind of funny. He didn't imagine anyone

could block Manza. He was a man among boys. That was the simple fact, but no one had made that clear before. Zeb bent under the center and put his hands on Jiler's butt. He looked up and down the line. He looked at Manza. Manza had green dashes under his eyes to help with the sunshine. The dashes made him look like a Marine of some sort.

On the count, the ball came into Zeb's hands, but before he could move Manza crushed him. It had happened impossibly fast. No one, Zeb figured, had touched Manza. If they *had* touched him and he had still gotten in so fast, then they were in for a long, long day.

Manza shot back to his feet. He held up his index finger and ran it beneath his eye as if he had a mote of dust there and needed to shake it away. *One* was the clear message. He planned to have plenty of tackles.

"All day, all day, all day," Manza yelled.

He jump-bumped with half his team. Zeb tossed the ball to the ref. They had lost four yards. It was lucky, Zeb knew, that he hadn't fumbled. Manza looked like a Christmas tree jump-bumping with elves.

"Same play," Zeb said back in the huddle. "And you got to block, people. We don't stand a chance unless you block. You have to lay something on him."

No one said anything. Zeb realized they were terrified. He thought maybe he should say something, try to break the spell, but it didn't seem the right moment. The moment would come, maybe, but it wasn't now. He called the play by number, gave a snap count, then followed the breaking team up to the line of scrimmage. Manza had moved. He now stood over center, the ridgepole of a building that extended out to the defensive ends. The kid had an enormous wingspan, Zeb saw. He really was like a comic-book villain. He was a nightmare monster come to life.

"Coming at you, QB. Coming at you," Manza said.

The line judge blew a whistle. He blew in a dozen short tweets, then shot in to put his foot on the ball.

"I want both captains here! I want them right here," the line judge said.

Dunham stepped forward. To Zeb's surprise, the captain for Merrymeeting was not Manza. It was a defensive back named Phillips. Zeb knew him from studying defensive tendencies. He knew the name, but that was about all. Phillips stood next to Dunham. His uniform looked crazy green.

"You boys listening to me? We're not going to be talking and taunting all game, do you hear me? We will flag for unsportsmanlike, bang-bang. Cut it out. Both teams, cut it out, starting right now. You are playing for the New Hampshire state championship. We don't need to wallow around like pigs in a puddle, do we? Are we clear, gentlemen?"

Dunham nodded. The line judge looked at Manza. Manza shrugged. Then the line judge trotted to one sideline and then the other and explained what he had outlined to the players. A few fans began to boo. It took too long. It killed the excitement. Zeb told his team to get back in the huddle. After all the emotion of the first play, suddenly the pace seemed leisurely. But the ref had been smart. The talking would have escalated. It was better to stop it early. That was good game management on the ref's part.

Zeb changed his mind about the play. He called a play-action pass. He would fake to Otzman, then bootleg past Manza. Then he would pull up and pass to Gray, the tight end, trailing across the middle of the field. It was a risky play because he would have no blocking on Manza. But he knew Manza would be slavering to hit someone and he would assume Zeb had handed the ball off. That was the percentage play to handoff. Zeb didn't feel like playing the percentages.

"We're running a boom pass. Gray get open. Fake hard, Dunham. Manza is going to come after you. I'm going to bootleg past him and you're going to be wide open, Gray."

"You got it," Gray said.

"Don't rush it. Delay and then drag open."

It was a good call. Daring, but good. Coming off the line judge's warning, both teams would be keyed up. That's what Zeb counted on. If he screwed up, Coach K would yank him. He would at least pull him out to talk to him. But Zeb didn't care. He hadn't come all this way to be timid.

The team broke. Manza had resumed his position at right defensive end. He didn't say anything, but his fingers still twitched. Zeb took his time coming to the line. Any delay would only get Manza more eager to crush something. That was the trick of it.

Zeb bent under Jiler and called the cadence. The ball snapped into his hands and he faked it to Otzman, putting his free hand into Otzman's gut and getting a tug as Otzman pretended to take the ball. The ball, though, rode on Zeb's hip, hidden, safe, and Zeb felt more than saw Manza flash past. He heard someone grunt and he kept going past, not revealing the ball yet, pretending calmness where he felt none. Then, like a flower opening in a time-lapse nature film, Zeb saw the field. He saw everything. He saw Gray slowly pretending to block, then scraping off and dragging across the center of the field. He saw the defensive backs charging in to crush Otzman. He heard someone yell "Ball" as if Otzman had fumbled, but Zeb ignored it and kept drifting. Here it was. Here was a play that could have been drawn up for his particular talents. He was good at hiding what he really understood, what he really meant, because that had been important growing up. So the fake to Otzman was a lie, a well-told lie, and his casual glance down the field compounded the falsehood. But then he saw Gray sprint open, crossing across the hash marks, the defensive back ignoring him. Zeb pulled up and felt his knee flex dangerously, but he couldn't worry about that now. He planted calmly and drew the ball back. At the same time, he had a faint understanding that the fake had played out and that *now, now, now,* everyone knew who had the ball. He felt Manza skimming down the line toward him, his steps thudding on the ground like a wild animal, a low moan emanating from his chest, while Zeb told himself to let it go, let it go smoothly, be silk, be the deer, and he brought his arm forward and threw a perfect spiral to Gray. It might have been his most beautiful pass, his purest throw, and it did not surprise him when Gray gathered it into his chest. Gray did not break stride and the crowd now went up and Zeb heard a large gasp, a cheer as the fans realized what had happened, and then Manza reached him.

The bridge of Manza's helmet caught Zeb under the right edge of his helmet and knocked it cleanly away. Zeb felt himself lifted and for an instant it was nearly fun. Manza's momentum carried them both up, like a great white shark lifting a sea lion into the air as it left the water. Zeb knew the moment couldn't last, knew he would suffer for the pleasure he experienced, but a distant part of him heard people cheering crazily now and he knew, suspected, believed, that Gray had reached the end zone.

Then pain. He felt Manza's weight drive him into the dirt and his full force crashed down on Zeb's frame, and Zeb felt his bones bow and spring back. In the weeks afterward, that particular tackle would cause newspaper columns and local sports talk shows to discuss whether there should be a size limit on high school athletes, because the discrepancy in size made the tackle appear incredibly brutal. And it was. As Zeb felt the dirt under him, he knew he had been hit as he had never been hit before. His helmet had launched across the line of scrimmage and Manza had landed on him, a huge huff of air coming out of him as he landed on Zeb. He wasn't vicious, Zeb understood. As soon as they landed, Manza sprang off him and extended a hand, ready to pull Zeb to his feet.

"You got us—nice move, Holloway. Nice. I'll give it to you."

Zeb held up an arm and let Manza pull him up. Sound seemed garbled and discordant. Then Zeb saw McCay holding out his helmet and someone else slapped him on the butt, and it dawned on Zeb slowly that Gray had scored, that he had run close to sixty yards on the second play from scrimmage in the New Hampshire state championship game. And he, Zeb Holloway, had called the play and thrown the pass to make it all happen.

He trotted to the sideline. He thought he might have suffered a concussion. He thought his off-side arm, his left arm, might be separated at the shoulder.

"Yeah, yeah, yeah," Coach Hoch yelled, slapping butts of anyone who came off the field. "That's what we're talking about. There we go! That's Raider football."

Coach K grabbed Zeb by the facemask. He stuck his face close and nodded. That was all. Then he let him go. Zeb wasn't sure where he was supposed to go now. His body felt ruined. Ironically, his knee felt fine.

"You okay? Jesus Christ, he hit the hell out of you, Zebby," Hawny said, his voice incredibly welcome. "Jesus, he pounded you."

"Help me sit down for a second, would you?"

"You okay?"

Zeb shook his head no. But it came out half yes, half no.

"You threw a touchdown pass!" Hawny said, guiding him to the bench. "On the second play from scrimmage."

"We can't block Manza. He's too big and too fast."

"I'm telling you, man, you laid it in there like a pro. You were chill out there! So chill!"

Zeb sat. He still couldn't think very well. He wondered if he could ask for smelling salts, something to clear his head, but that would trigger all sorts of questions. Better to be quiet about it, he concluded. He wasn't coming out of the game no matter what.

Gray came over and sat down beside him. Gray looked happy and sweaty and excited. He held out his hand for a knuckle-bump. Zeb knuckle-bumped him with his right hand. He wasn't sure he could lift his left arm, the one Manza had landed on.

"That was so slick," Gray said. "So cool."

"Good play," Zeb said. "I thought they might bite."

"They bit. They bit hard."

"Give him a second," Hawny said. "He got the wind knocked out of him."

Gray was a good guy. He nodded and took off. Zeb looked up

at the sky. The mackerel clouds had given way to a greater darkness. Even as he looked, a piddling rain began. It fell in a misty glow, the weak November sun no match for the haze the rain carried with it.

At halftime it was 13 to 7 in favor of Merrymeeting. Merrymeeting had scored one touchdown and kicked two field goals. They had a good kicker, Zeb knew, an All-State kid named Hynoski. For the Rumney offensive's part, they hadn't done anything. Zero. Trotting off the field in the increased rain, Zeb realized the offense had not put up a single first down. It had been laughable, really. No one could block Manza. He ran around and did whatever he wanted, and most of the players were frightened of him. No one would say it, but Zeb knew it to be true. Manza was the secret to Merrymeeting's success just as T.T. had been the secret to Rumney's winning season. Merrymeeting still had its star and Rumney did not. The touchdown pass, Zeb knew, had been a fluke. Merrymeeting wouldn't bite again so easily.

Zeb slowed when they reached the concrete walkway to the lockers. Everything had turned slick. The rain lived right on the edge of becoming ice and sleet. Deer season, Zeb thought as he ducked into the warmth of the locker room. Until he was inside, Zeb didn't realize how cold he had become.

"Hydrate, hydrate, hydrate," Mrs. Gilmore shouted over the milling voices. "Just because it's wet and cold doesn't mean you don't need to hydrate. Get some electrolytes inside you. Drink . . . no excuses. See me if you have an injury. Let someone know, people."

Coach Steve, down from the spotting booth, grabbed Zeb. Zeb

wasn't exactly in the mood for more coaching at that moment. He wanted to get warm and sit. But Coach Steve pulled him aside and showed him a series of photographs he had taken with his iPad.

"You see what they're doing? They're stacking Manza on the weak side, then bringing the linebacker on a scrape most plays. They're giving us too many people to block. We need to screen them and to run draws . . . misdirection."

Zeb nodded. He suddenly felt exhausted. His left arm hung limply at his side. He could move it, but barely. His knee felt okay, but his ribs pained him when he breathed.

"I need to sit down, Coach," Zeb said when Coach Steve had finished explaining about the defensive alignment. "I need a minute."

"You're doing fine, Zeb," Coach Steve said. "That pass to Gray was money. Beautiful execution. Top-notch."

Zeb nodded. He found a seat near his locker. He felt bone tired, but he also knew that he couldn't be beaten. Not really. He was from Redtree Road and people didn't give up on Redtree Road. If you gave up there, you crumpled. You had nothing behind you. So he stood and went around the locker room. He knuckle-bumped everyone he could. He hurt, but that was okay. *We can do this,* he said. He said it to himself as much as to the other players. He said it so often he began to believe it.

Dino circulated with orange slices and water bottles. He looked to be in a full sweat. Zeb sat back on the bench beside his locker and took an orange slice when it was his turn. He put it in his mouth and sucked on the goodness. He had never tasted anything better. Mrs. Gilmore squatted in front of him.

"How you doing, Zeb? You okay?"

Zeb nodded.

"That was a heck of a tackle on that pass play. Are you sure you're all right?"

She looked at his eyes. Zeb nodded. He didn't trust his voice exactly.

"And your knee . . . how is that holding up?"

"It's fine. Thanks."

"Let me see your eyes. Do you have a headache?"

"I'm fine, Mrs. Gilmore."

She studied him. Zeb forced himself to look at her evenly.

Coach Steve called for the offense to circle him next to a marker board. Zeb tried to follow the talk, but Coach Steve's description of the defensive schemes run by Merrymeeting did not sink into Zeb's consciousness. It was too much, too technical, and it skipped over the simple truth that no one could block Manza.

"But we're not blocking," Coach Steve said finally. "It all starts and ends with blocking. If you don't stick your helmet in Manza's chest, then we're not going anywhere. I can't give you balls, boys. I can't give my testicles to you. No one can. You need to suck it up and man up and do what needs to be done. Do you follow me?"

"Yes," a few kids answered.

"Do you?"

"Yes!"

It was louder, but it still wasn't great. Coach Steve told them to hit the john and then gather for Coach K. Coach K wanted to address them. Coach K, he implied, was not happy with the first-half effort.

"You okay?" Hawny whispered.

Zeb realized he was zoning out.

"You got a concussion or something, man. You should tell Mrs. Gilmore."

"I'll be okay. Just had my bell rung. I'm okay."

"It's not worth scrambling your brain over. The game, I mean. It's just a game."

Zeb didn't know about that. He didn't know if the game wasn't something more important than Hawny could guess. Coach Adams at Emporia was going to watch the video. The game meant that. It also meant he had the guts to go the distance. Corny but true. Zeb understood he would never remove himself from the game. T.T. had superior talent, but Zeb's guts weren't a backup to anyone's. That much he knew.

Thirty minutes to go. Thirty minutes left.

Dino came in and reported to anyone who would listen that the rain had picked up. It was raining hard, sleeting. It was nasty out, Dino said. It was slick, the ground was slick, the air was slick, the world was slick. Apparently the police were concerned about people driving after the game.

"Okay, boys," Coach K said. "Okay, settle in. We only have a minute. We're doing fine. We've got another whole half to play and we've always been a strong second-half team. We own the last quarter. We always have. No reason to change that now."

Zeb tried to listen. He really did. But whatever Coach K wanted to say didn't work anymore. Zeb felt funny. He felt as if his skin glowed or his head clouded or some combination of both. Maybe he did have a concussion. That was possible. The world seemed far away somehow. He deliberately sat forward and put his hands on his knees, trying to concentrate, but all that registered was the warmth of the locker room, the pure goodness of feeling his toes.

". . . give him time," Coach K concluded, and Zeb realized the coach had been talking about him. About having time to pass. About blocking Manza.

"Thirty minutes to prove you're champions," Coach K finished. "Do you have it in you, boys? Do you have it in your hearts? Now let's go. This is Rumney football! This is Raider football. Now let's take it to them . . ."

But before they could roar their agreement, Zeb heard a louder roar come from the Merrymeeting locker room. When Rumney shouted, it sounded like a half echo of the Merrymeeting cheer. Then it was time to go out again. Zeb stood. Coach Steve stood in the doorway and knuckle-bumped everyone who passed. Zeb knuckle-bumped with him. Coach Steve looked him in the eye and nodded encouragement.

The field, Zeb realized, had changed. It had changed a lot. It had *fished up,* just as Uncle Pushee would have predicted. Zeb took in deep breaths. The weather would be his friend, he knew. Weather didn't bother him. Weather didn't bother people raised on Redtree Road.

"Come on, let's go, let's go!" Dunham yelled.

He danced backwards onto the field and swatted at people as they ran past. Zeb didn't want to be swatted but he accepted Dunham's smack. Hawny appeared with a football and offered to warm him up. Zeb nodded. Throwing might center him, he thought. Throwing always did. He cranked his arm and tossed a soft lob to Hawny. Hawny caught it, tucked it under his arm, and lobbed the ball back.

As Zeb threw again he pictured his father, Lawrence, vaulting the fence. He pictured him landing and pausing a second, wondering whether he should go or stay. He pictured him putting one hand back on the fence, considering what it would take to reverse his course, then smiling—the smile the photo had captured—and continuing on, no longer looking behind, no longer knowing the way back to his son. He pictured his mother watching out the window as her husband, her son's father, decided against staying. He pictured her not crying, not doing anything but tightening her hand on the windowsill, her pain too great to voice.

Two minutes into the second half, Zeb realized the game was over. Maybe it had always been over, he couldn't say, but it became clear when Merrymeeting marched down the field and punched in a second touchdown: 19–7. Then the extra point, with Hynoski kicking it a mile through the uprights: 20–7.

It was not an insurmountable lead, exactly, but with Manza on the defense, it was unlikely Rumney could score more than another touchdown, if that. The knowledge seemed to descend on the stadium from up in the sky. Zeb felt it sink into the sidelines, even into the coaches, though no one could admit it. Merrymeeting was too good.

Zeb called a screen left to Otzman on the first offensive play of the second half. Manza knocked it down before Zeb could loft it over his head. The play looked stupid, Zeb knew. It looked overmatched from the snap.

Zeb was preparing to call the second play when Jimbo suddenly appeared and told Zeb he was in to substitute. Zeb looked for a long count at him, but he realized Jimbo wasn't to blame. No one was to blame. Things just went a certain way and that's all there was to it.

Zeb trotted off the field. He heard a smattering of applause. He realized, as he came to the sideline, that he would be part of the story in the papers the next day. *Sub QB not able to bring T.T.'s magic.* Something like that. Zeb turned and watched the play. Jimbo took off on a sprint right, faked a pass, and then tucked the ball under his arm and ran. He gained seven yards. It was one of the biggest plays of the day not counting the long touchdown pass.

Someone in the stands blew a long, loud blast on an air horn.

Coach K came over and put his arm around Zeb's waist.

"Let's see if he can shake it up. We need to get something started, Zeb."

"Yes, sir."

"You did fine. Don't get too cold. I'm going to send you back in in a little bit. Get a jacket."

Zeb didn't want a jacket. He wondered now if the whole team had been waiting for him to be pulled. Maybe they had seen the lack of offense as his fault all along. He didn't know. The offense sucked. That was the long and short of it.

Jimbo ran again and this time he fumbled. Merrymeeting recovered. They had the ball on the Rumney thirty-yard line. It took the refs a long time to untangle the pile. When they did, Phillips, the Merrymeeting captain, stood up and pounded his chest. He had the ball in his right hand.

"Fuck a duck," Coach Hoch yelled and slammed down his headset. "I told that stupid bastard to hold on to the ball no matter what. Jesus H. Christ."

"Defense," Freckles the linebacker called. "Come on, D. Pick 'em up. Next man up. Let's go to work."

But Zeb could have predicted the long run that happened

next. On the second play, a tiny running back, a quick little splinter named James, slipped around the left end and went the distance. No one touched him, really. He did a celebration dance in the end zone and the refs blew their whistles and flagged him for unsportsmanlike conduct, but no one cared. It was 26 to 7, and the third quarter was almost over. Hynoski kicked the extra point lazily. The ball ticked off the upright and jumped through. All over the stadium, people laughed.

"You're back in, Zeb," Coach Hoch said as the teams lined up for the kickoff. "You loose? Make sure you're loose."

"Yes, sir."

Zeb didn't watch the kickoff. He went to find Hawny instead.

"You're coming in with me," Zeb said. "Go in and play for Gray. Don't check with the coaches, just come in. Stay beside me."

"Are you kidding me?"

Zeb shook his head. Hawny wore a long jacket. He shucked it off and put on his helmet. He dug his mouthpiece out of his waistband. His uniform looked absurdly clean. Zeb didn't worry about Gray. He could tell Gray it was a special play, one they had practiced secretly. It was just one play, anyway. It wasn't going to change the game one way or the other. Everyone knew the game was over. All the rest was simply pretend.

When Haynes, the return man, got tackled on the twenty-seven-yard line, Zeb trotted onto the field. Hawny trotted beside him. If anyone noticed, they didn't say anything. Zeb told Gray to jump out, that Hawny had come in for a special play.

"What the fuck is this all about?" McCay said.

"Secret weapon," Zeb said and nearly laughed.

He called the same play he had called for Gray, the scoring

play from the first half. On the snap he faked again to Otzman, but this time no one bought it. Zeb had to run to avoid a tackle. Fortunately, Manza was on the other side, so Zeb was able to escape momentarily. He picked up Hawny's uniform easily enough and launched the ball in his general direction just before getting nailed. He doubted he had come close with the throw. He felt his ribs spring again as he fell to the ground with two Merrymeeting players driving him down.

Coach K sent in Jimbo and Gray and subbed Zeb and Hawny out. Coach K pointed at Zeb as soon as he crossed the sideline and then pointed to the bench. Zeb nodded and looked up at the rain falling. It fell and couldn't make up its mind whether to be snow or not.

The final score was 30–7. Zeb lined up with the rest of his team and passed down the ranks of the Merrymeeting players slapping hands and saying congratulations. Now that it was over, they did not seem like bad guys. In fact, they seemed a little embarrassed by how easily they had won. Or maybe, Zeb considered, they knew the outcome might have been different if T.T. had played. T.T. threw a shadow over everything.

When Zeb came to Manza, he realized Manza didn't recognize him, or didn't care to recognize him. Manza passed by and kept looking to one side, probably to say hello to parents or friends. Merrymeeting was the New Hampshire state champ. Saying "Good game" was merely a formality.

Zeb took his time going back to the locker room. He felt he had been largely to blame for the loss. Yes, Merrymeeting proved the superior team, but Zeb wondered if he couldn't have figured a way to even the contest a little. Maybe not. It was over now and he felt the cold, the all-day cold, living like a foggy mist inside his bones.

He had nearly made it to the locker room when Arthur stepped up and extended his hand. He wore a gray watch cap and a red plaid jacket. His face looked pinched with cold. His nostrils stretched too wide.

"Good game, Zeb," Arthur said. "You gave it your best."

"Thanks, Arthur."

"That first pass was really something."

"Well, that's about all we did all day . . ."

Someone blew an air horn nearby. Merrymeeting fans. Zeb saw three of the Rumney cheerleaders—not Stella—scoot by, their arms wrapped around themselves for warmth. Now that the game was over, the fact of the weather became more essential.

"Your mother will be very proud," Arthur said. "Very proud."

"Thanks, Arthur."

Arthur smiled. For a moment Zeb wondered if Arthur was going to try to hug him. But he demonstrated good sense. He patted Zeb's shoulder and Zeb understood he was released. Zeb followed the stream of players and fans going toward the locker room. He found himself next to Dunham, whose eyes looked red from crying. Zeb didn't blame him for crying. Zeb felt emotional too, but he couldn't pinpoint what emotion ruled the others.

When he made it inside the locker room, Dino handed him a note.

"From a girl," Dino said. "She said it was important."

The note said, *Let's go look at the ocean.* It wasn't signed, but Zeb knew it was from Ferron. He felt his heart lift and he looked around quickly, as if she might somehow be in the locker room. That was ridiculous, of course, but he felt something warm and correct enter his blood. Ferron. It felt as though he had just received the best present in the world.

Hawny came up and knuckle-bumped him.

"Thanks," Hawny said. "Now I can die a happy man. I got into a game."

"Coach K wasn't happy about it."

"Coach K can blow me."

Zeb smiled. Then he laughed. Hawny could always make things funny.

"Ferron is here. I'm going to get a ride with her, I think."

"You're not going on the bus?"

"I don't think so."

"I thought she wasn't coming to the game."

"That's what I thought too."

"She's loving herself some Zebby the Zebra."

Zeb laughed again. Soft, but he laughed. Life didn't end at the finish of a football game. Hawny always knew things like that.

Zeb undressed and took a shower. His body ached. His head still felt buzzy. But now it was over. What was going to happen had now happened. He had stood up to everything that came at him. He had thrown a touchdown pass. He hadn't fumbled or thrown an interception. He hadn't given the game away. Maybe he hadn't beaten the champion, but he had stayed on his feet and played to the end. He hadn't given up. He would never give up, he knew. That was something the game had revealed to him.

Coach K came in then and called the team to order. Zeb finished dressing quietly as the coach talked.

"Boys, we got beat fair and square today. Today, Merrymeeting was the better team. But one loss should not diminish what you accomplished this season. It really shouldn't. We couldn't be more proud of you . . . the whole community could not be more proud of you. I want to congratulate you personally on a great season. Take the loss like sportsmen and gentlemen. Be generous in your praise of Merrymeeting. You only diminish us, what we have accomplished, if you go down the path of sour grapes."

That was it. Coach Hoch stepped in and told people to let Dino know if they did not intend to go back on the bus. Fifteen minutes until departure. Shake a leg. Get a move on. The season had ended.

"I'm going to go look for her," Zeb told Hawny. "See you later."

"Good game, man."

"Thanks. Did my throw to you come anywhere close?"

"Not by about twenty yards. It sucked. You threw a freaking duck out there."

"Sorry."

"You threw it to me, Zeb. That's what I'll remember."

As soon as he stepped out of the door he saw Stella and T.T. They stood side by side, T.T. balanced on his crutches, Stella in wind pants and a heavy cheerleading windbreaker.

"Tough game," T.T. said, swinging closer on his crutches.

Stella hung back, as if the piece of asphalt they had been standing on belonged to them and needed to be reserved.

"Well, we could have used you. I didn't have much luck."

"When you scored on that first drive I thought you might be on to something. Then it kind of dried up."

"That's an understatement."

"We had a good run anyway," T.T. said. "We got to states."

"How did the surgery turn out?"

T.T. shrugged.

"I tell everyone it's great, but who knows? I'll tell you what. It hurts like crazy almost all the time. It hurts like nothing I've ever felt before. The muscles are all shot around it."

"Did the doctors give you a good prognosis?"

T.T. shrugged again.

"I don't put all my faith in doctors. If the Lord wills it, I'll play again. If He doesn't, I'll accept my life on His terms."

"Okay, good. I hope it works out."

"I doubt I'll see much of you after today. I'm heading back to Texas with my family. I wanted to see the game. We had some stuff to clear up back here too. I'll see you around, Zeb. Don't take the game too hard."

"I won't."

Zeb knuckle-bumped him. T.T. swung back toward Stella. Zeb felt he could breathe again. Looking around the parking lot, he spotted Ferron. She leaned against the Volvo's driver-side door, writing something on what looked like a sketchpad.

He walked toward her, aware his body had started to clench. His knee throbbed and he couldn't clear his head. His hair felt rigid and cold against his scalp and now and then a bead of moisture released from the tendrils and dripped down his neck. He should have dried his hair better, he realized.

"You guys lost," Ferron said, looking up from her sketchpad. "That's not good."

"Not good at all."

"I'm sorry. I know it meant a lot to you."

"It did."

"Did you lose by a ton?"

"Didn't you watch the game?"

She shook her head. She wore a pink cap pulled down tight over her head. She looked cozy.

"I don't like football," she said, folding the sketchbook closed. "And I worried you might get hurt. I didn't want to see you get hurt."

"Do you still want to go see the ocean?"

"Is it a good idea to see it? I mean now, after everything?"

"Sure. It would feel like the right thing to do, actually. I could stand to get away for a minute. I'm tired of football."

"Let's go, then."

He held the door for her, then limped around to the passenger side and threw his bag in the back. He climbed in. The car felt warm and smelled like her perfume. She looked beautiful sitting behind the steering wheel.

"I am sorry you lost, Zeb," she said when she started the car. "Sincerely. It's hard to work at something and then not quite get what you had hoped out of it."

Zeb shrugged. He felt sleepy. The warmth of the car hit like a narcotic. Until this moment he hadn't realized how exhausted he felt.

"I did my best. Merrymeeting was better than we were."

"That happens. Sometimes you can't win no matter what. Sometimes it lines up against you."

He nodded. She reached over and grabbed his hand. He squeezed her fingers. Her touch did more for him than anything else he could think of at that moment. It surprised him to know that no matter what happened in the world, he could still hold her hand. That didn't have to change. That could be an anchor. He had never felt that before.

"What would you have done if I had said no to going to the ocean?"

"I would have gone anyway. I go all the time. I was in the mood to see it. How do you feel? I saw you limping. Did they hurt you?"

"They knocked me around pretty good."

"It's kind of sexy. I wish they had broken your nose. I like a twisted nose on a boy."

"I'll try to arrange that next time I play."

"You don't have to break it just for me. But I wouldn't mind if it happened."

"Okay."

"A broken nose. That does it for me."

"Noted."

"Do you need to sleep, Zeb? You could sleep for ten minutes or so. We'll go out to the Great Island Common, okay? We can pull right up and look out at the sea."

"Maybe I'll close my eyes."

"You should. You won't die, though, will you? I'd hate to pull up to the ocean and find you had kicked the bucket."

He smiled.

"I'm okay."

"I'll wake you when we get there."

His phone woke him. He dug it out of his pocket, momentarily confused about his location. Then it came to him. He was in

Ferron's car at a beach in New Hampshire. He looked out the window. The sun had started its afternoon slide. Before long it would be dark. The ocean stretched like a pigeon's neck reaching to peck, then pull back, then peck again.

"Hi, Mom," he said.

"Where are you, honey?"

"At the beach with Ferron."

"Arthur called and told me all about the game, Zeb. I'm so sorry."

"It's okay, Mom."

"He said you played very well. He said you did your best."

"I did, I guess. I did what I could. I didn't hold anything back."

"Well, that's what counts, honey. You know I love you no matter what, don't you?"

"I know, Mom."

"You know, your uncle Pushee stopped over and said he listened to the game. It was the first time he volunteered to talk to me in I don't know how long. It was as if we had stopped talking just the other day. He's a strange man."

Zeb didn't know what to say to that. He watched the ocean roll in and out.

"How's your knee, honey?"

"I'm okay, Mom."

"I'm glad to hear that."

"How are you, Mom?" he asked suddenly, not even sure what he meant by the question.

"How do you mean, Zeb?"

"I mean, I realize you go to work every day and you never

really complain. I don't know. You're playing a game, too, in a way."

"I never thought of it like that."

"I learned a lot from you, Mom. Watching you keep going."

He heard her swallow on the other end of the line. He wondered how you could live next to someone all your life and never say what you mean to say.

"I have to get back to my tables," she said. "I love you, honey. You're the best son a mom could have."

"Thanks, Mom."

"Your life is going to be good, Zeb. Better than mine. Just keep going forward."

"I will, Mom."

"Okay, sweetie. Love you."

"Love you too, Mom."

She clicked off. He put his phone away. Moving to open the car door, he felt he had to climb back inside his body. Climbing inside it brought pain, though, and he had to move his limbs carefully to let them loosen. He closed the door behind him and looked again at the sea.

He spotted Ferron alone on the beach. He walked toward her slowly, feeling his body trying to free itself. He had played well. He knew that now. He knew he could watch the film of the loss and not feel ashamed. There was no dishonor in what had happened.

When Ferron saw him approaching, she stopped whatever she was doing and waved. It was a full wave, hand over her head, happy. He felt himself smiling.

Zeb watched her and felt something like love climb up his body and nearly choke him. When he reached her, she slipped under his arm. She wore no shoes. He looked down at her feet and saw she had been making a design in the sand.

"Aren't you freezing?" he whispered.

"Yes. Totally."

"It's cold out here."

"This is life, Zeb. This is the good part."

"I don't know this part very well."

"I know you don't. I know that about you."

"I think we should stay by each other for a while."

"So do I."

The wind brought a gull close to them. He took a few good breaths. The sea smelled old and familiar and entirely new. That was a confusing thing, but he understood it was true.

"Something changed today," he said close to her ear. "I don't even know what it is, but it did. I can feel it."

"Good, Zeb."

"You're part of it, but it's other things too. I thought life had to go one way but now I see maybe it doesn't."

"Okay."

"I must sound like an idiot."

"You sound like anything but an idiot."

On the drive home, he was quiet, thinking of his parents and of his future.

"I don't think I was much company," he said. "I apologize. I guess the game beat me up more than I knew."

"You were tired, Zeb. I probably should have let you go back on the bus."

"I'm glad you didn't. We saw the ocean."

She nodded. He took her hand and kissed the back of it, then climbed out. He grabbed his bag from the back seat and then leaned inside again.

"I live here in that camper," he said, nodding his head to indicate the Sunline. "This bigger house is my uncle's house. My mom and I live over there. Sometimes I let people think I live in my uncle's house, but I don't."

She nodded.

"We do our best," he said. "I thought you should know."

She reached across suddenly and hugged him. He felt her crying more than saw it. He kissed her cheek and she pulled back behind the wheel. He closed the door softly and walked toward the camper thinking he would need to make a fire, need to make it warm for his mother's return.

TURN THE PAGE FOR AN EXCERPT OF *WHIPPOORWILL.*

"A bighearted, gorgeous, timely champion for empathy, kindness, and common courtesy." —MATTHEW QUICK, *New York Times* best-selling author of *The Silver Linings Playbook* and *Forgive Me, Leonard Peacock*

★ "The narrative adeptly portrays longing and belonging, and the heartbreak and hope of not only the human condition but the canine one as well. Monninger revitalizes the boy-and-dog trope in this sweet novel." —*SCHOOL LIBRARY JOURNAL,* starred review

★ "Narrator Clair is absolutely believable as the girl who's stable yet also negotiating her own loss." —*THE BULLETIN,* starred review

ONE

AT NIGHT I could always hear him.

He turned on his chain, trying to find a comfortable spot, and you heard a moment of quiet as if the whole world waited to see what he would do. Then the chain chinked just a little and you could hear him huff and then fall into his dog box, the heavy thump of his body on the boards, the chain lifting a notch to accommodate his neck.

Sometimes he whined and I could hardly stand it.

It turned minus thirty one night and he still stayed outside.

"It's New Hampshire and it's late February," my dad said. "What do you expect?"

He sat at the kitchen table fooling around with his motorcycle parts. He had his big beard then, his winter beard, and he hardly had cheeks for all the whiskers. He wore a quilted flannel shirt and red suspenders. A pair of tortoiseshell glasses from Walmart perched on the end of his nose so he could see one of the parts.

"He shouldn't be outside," I said, looking out the door at the porch thermometer.

"No, I guess not," he agreed, "but we can't start a war with the neighbors."

"The heck with them," I said. "I hate them. We shouldn't care about them if they can't bother to care about the dog."

"That's no way for a sixteen-year-old girl to talk, Clair. We can't judge other people so easily."

"He could die."

"All things die," he said, not looking my way.

He meant my mother, I knew, but he was being poetic.

That night, in the cold, I threw some leftover breakfast sausages to Wally. They landed close enough to his pole so that he could get them, but he didn't even respond. The snow had covered his back legs, and for a long time I stood watching, trying to tell if he had frozen to death. He looked back at me. His two nostrils streamed puffs of white air. White air, white night, white moon.

A black lab named Wally.

* * *

A dog is a social animal. Tying a dog out on a pole by himself is about the cruelest thing you can do to a canine. Dogs live in packs and some scientists say they care more about other members in their pack than they do about humans. They only care about humans if you become one of their pack.

Instead of tying a dog out by himself, it would be kinder to shoot him.

My bedroom looks out on the Stewarts' property. I could see over the stockade fence that separated our cruddy yards, and I watched Wally from the time he arrived in mid-February. The Stewarts are what people in New Hampshire call Whippoorwills. It's a north country name for trash hounds. The Stewarts have at least five cars in their backyard in various states of disrepair, two half-beat Farmall tractors, both spotted orange, a snowmobile so rusted, it looks like it wants to grow into the earth, an aboveground swimming pool that has collapsed on the north end so that it lies crushed and broken and useless, a trampoline that works, a stumpy white pine, at least five truck axles, and a dozen chicken pens, built above ground to house rabbits and a couple of guinea hens.

Wally was one more piece of junk.

* * *

We aren't much better.

My dad, John T. Taylor, is a wannabe biker. He has a Harley Softail, which, if you know anything about motorcycles, is supposed to be a big deal. He rides with a pack of guys called the Devil's Tongue, and they aren't as tough as they'd like to be, but they can intimidate the local New Hampshire people when they thunder up and down Route 25. You can feel them in the ground when they pass, and they always remind me of locusts or buffalo when I see them traveling. If you know who they are, though, they don't scare you a bit, because you understand my dad, for instance, is a heat and plumbing guy, and the Devil's Tongue leader is a little weirdo named Jebby. Jebby looks like a rhinoceros, all shoulders and neck, except he is only five foot four and pigeon-toed. Jebby is a rural mail carrier, which means he drives around on dirt roads shoving mail into boxes. He has a blinking light on his Jeep, and he eats turkey sandwiches at the same highway turnout every day of his working life at 12:10 sharp. That's where my dad sometimes finds him to talk about rides. The other guys are more or less the same, tradesmen and grease guys, and you can't be around them without understanding they sort of like the idea of being in a motorcycle gang, but they could never commit to being in a real one like the Hells Angels or the Iron Horsemen. After Mom died about three years ago, the motorcycle became more central in my dad's life, and he's always working on it, one way or the other, with the small kitchen television blasting and the breakfast table covered with newspapers and machine parts. Jebby comes by sometimes, and so do some of the others, and what they seem to like most is *talking* about riding. They rhapsodize about riding without helmets, and about Bike Week in June down at the Weirs in Laconia, New Hampshire, and part of me can't stand to listen to their ridiculous talk, and another part of me is glad my father has someone to talk to. He's kind of a loner—well, we both are—and sometimes it feels like we are two dice rattling around in this cruddy old house, and that when my mom died, she gave us a great big shake and we've been rolling ever since.

For what it's worth, my mom, Sylvia, was what people call flighty, when they're being kind, and undependable, when they're being mean. She was a part-time art teacher at some of the elementary schools here in New Hampshire. She drove around in an old Subaru station wagon and went to different schools and worked with the kids. She specialized in found art. Found art is when you take old junk and make something more interesting out of it. *The junk suggests its shape to you,* she'd say. What that really meant was the porch of our colonial house was so jammed with crud, you could barely squeeze through it, but Mom didn't notice. She was always going to yard sales or buying some cheap junk at Second Comings, the church secondhand store. It was a disease with her, really, like a hoarder who uses other people's discards to seal herself off from the world. Walling herself off, living way down inside herself, constituted my mom's real art.